"I have to deal with this myself."

Paul shook his head slowly. "You need someone to look after you. The father of the baby is dead, and I am here. So why not marry me?"

There was a long silence. It all seemed too easy, too convenient. It wasn't fair to burden Paul with someone else's child. He might regret it later, resent the child and blame her for it. She would never forgive herself.

"Paul...every time I see you looking at me I think about how the baby's not yours, and...."

"I wish it were mine," he said with sudden violence. "I wish to God it were!"

Kristen straightened in her chair. "See? That's what I mean! It's not your baby—it never can be! You'll hate me for it for the rest of your life!"

"That is not what I meant...."

These books may be available at your local bookseller.

Don't miss any of our special offers. Write to us at the
following address for information on our newest releases.

Harlequin Reader Service
P.O. Box 52040, Phoenix, AZ 85072-2040
Canadian address: P.O. Box 2800, Postal Station A,
5170 Yonge St., Willowdale, Ont.   M2N 6J3

KAREN VAN DER ZEE

staying close

Harlequin Books

TORONTO • NEW YORK • LONDON
AMSTERDAM • PARIS • SYDNEY • HAMBURG
STOCKHOLM • ATHENS • TOKYO • MILAN

Harlequin Presents first edition June 1985
ISBN 0-373-10798-6

Original hardcover edition published in 1984
by Mills & Boon Limited

CHAPTER ONE

Two days before Kristin was due to leave for Australia she heard that Rick was dead.

She was busy wrapping Christmas presents when a friend came to her apartment to tell her the news. After he had left, she sat in the middle of all the bright clutter of paper and ribbon and string, numb with shock. It didn't seem possible. Less than a week ago Rick had been here in this room, sitting next to her on the shabby couch, telling her he was leaving for Tunisia to work on an archaeological dig. Saying goodbye.

She closed her eyes, trying to push away the memory of that night, yet knowing she would never forget it.

She didn't know how long she sat there, staring blindly at the gold and silver wrapping paper while tears slid silently down her face.

Rick with the happy grin and the laughing eyes was dead. She couldn't comprehend it. It was impossible. *Impossible!* Rick, so young, so healthy, so full of life and joy . . . how could it be? And why? *Why?*

Her thoughts ran back in time, recalling memories of those first few awful months away from home, alone at the university. When she had first arrived at the huge campus three years ago she had felt a crushing fear. At home she had known everybody; here she knew no one. All those strange faces and no one to talk to. She had never felt so lonely in her life. As she had grown up in a small town and attended a high school with only four hundred students, the sheer number of people milling around the university campus had frightened her. Then, out of those countless, nameless faces, Rick had appeared like some guardian angel, and ever since, for the last three years, he had been her friend. She had dreaded the thought of him leaving, but it had been inevitable. He had just received his Master's degree, found the job he wanted and was looking forward to going abroad. She had been happy for him.

But she had never thought that their farewells would be so cruelly final.

And in the far recesses of her mind hovered a shadow of fear.

It was a long way from Oregon, U.S.A., to Australia, and by the time the plane touched down in Sydney, Kristin was exhausted.

She had never heard of spraying a plane before allowing the passengers to disembark. Fascinated, she watched as two giant males dressed in white shorts, knee socks and dress shoes (she had never seen that combination of garments worn together before) marched down the two aisles, a can of insecticide in each hand, spraying up in the air above the passengers' heads.

The captain explained that since Australia is an island, the flora and fauna are particularly vulnerable, and the introduction of foreign insects is potentially dangerous. Kristin visualised armies of alien bugs and germs ready to march out of the plane in microscopic multitudes to conquer Australia, wiping out entire crops and destroying herds of animals. Suspiciously she examined the bottom of her shoes, wondering what was hiding there waiting to spread death and disaster.

She straightened and watched the men as they progressed down the aisle, wondering why grown-up men would wear knee socks. She grinned at herself. No doubt other surprises were awaiting her in this foreign land.

She was looking forward to seeing her mother again. She lived in Sydney now with her newly acquired Australian husband, and Kristin had not seen her for eight months. She didn't even know the house her mother lived in now; all her life only one house had been home to her, and it was strange to think it was no longer theirs.

The spraying over, the passengers began to shuffle their way out of the plane, and Kristin followed impatiently.

Passport check, baggage claim, Customs clearance— it all seemed to take forever, but finally Kristin made it to the arrival hall and found herself face to face with her mother. She looked better than she had in years— younger and happier. Love, apparently, did this to you. They hugged and kissed and laughed as people milled around them. And then there was Uncle John, as he had asked her to call him, smiling broadly and hugging her warmly. Yes, it would be nice to spend the holidays here. Nice too, because of the lovely summer weather. December! She couldn't believe it. Sunshine and flowers and green grass and tanned people dressed in light clothes. She had left Oregon behind in the freezing cold and icy winds of winter, and now, only hours later, she found herself in the middle of summer. Such a strange feeling it was.

They drove through the city to Gordon, the North Shore suburb of Sydney where her mother now lived. It was a peaceful, quiet place with tree-lined streets of beautiful houses, rich green lawns and flowering shrubs.

They finally turned into a narrow drive fringed with flowers and blooming hydrangeas and stopped in front of a house made of mellow pinkish-beige brick. The brick, Uncle John said, was sandstock, handmade, and the same as the original brick used by the early settlers.

Kristin loved the house, its floors of cypress pine, the panelled walls, the large windows overlooking the yard all around the house. The kitchen, cosy, comfortable and convenient, was her mother's pride. Uncle John had remodelled it just for her right after they were married.

Kristin looked at her mother's shining eyes. At forty-three she was still a beautiful woman, with her slim figure, her curly auburn hair and her clear grey eyes. 'You're happy here, aren't you, Mom?' Kristin asked.

Her mother laughed, making a helpless gesture with her hand. 'What can I say? I love the man. He's wonderful!' She paused, her eyes serious as they scanned Kristin's face. 'And you?' she asked softly.

Kristin shrugged lightly. 'I'm fine.' She looked out the window, hesitating. She swallowed hard. 'Rick died last week,' she said tonelessly.

'Oh, my God!' Her mother stared at her in shock. 'What happened?'

'Some freak accident on an archaeological dig in Tunisia.'

'Tunisia?'

'He'd just gone there—his first real job. He was so happy about it.'

They looked at each other in silence.

'I'm sorry, Kristin,' her mother said at last.

'Yes. It's so ... so hard to understand. It seems so senseless. I keep thinking it's some awful mistake.'

'Yes.' Her mother studied Kristin's face. 'Are you all right?' she asked then, and Kristin nodded.

'Yes, I'm all right.' She smiled faintly and turned and slowly walked into the living room.

On one of the walls hung a large mounted photograph, a picture so arresting that Kristin stood in front of it for many minutes. Massive, forbidding-looking rocky cliffs jutted up to a cloudless blue sky. Every crack and crevice showed clear and sharp in the light. At the bottom in the sand sat a tiny, naked child, arms raised and sand flowing from its hands. Light caught the shiny hair and the falling grains of sand. The contrast between the small, smiling child and the massive cliffs rearing up behind it was stunning.

'It's one of Paul's,' her mother said. 'He's so good, his pictures make you think and feel things you never thought possible.'

Paul. One of Uncle John's sons. The other one's name was Scott.

Kristin slept an exhausted sleep that night in a yellow room with the white and yellow striped curtains covering the windows that were left open to let in the warm night air.

She awoke to the sound of birds. Through the open window a light breeze puffed the curtains. For a few minutes she lay still, luxuriating in the peaceful sounds coming from outside. Even the birds sounded different here. Well, they were different, weren't they? Australian birds. Her brain was not in gear yet. She took a deep breath. The air in the room felt clean and fresh. She stretched and relaxed, letting out a deep sigh. She hadn't slept like this for ages, so deep and restful and dreamless. For the first time she hadn't dreamed about Rick. Hurriedly she pushed the thought away. Not now. She didn't want to think about it now; it didn't help.

As she got out of bed her eyes searched the room for her robe. It was draped over a chair, and she wrapped it around and belted it. She looked at her watch. Ten o'clock. Ten! The bathroom was across the hall. She opened the door and stepped out—and found herself looking straight at the stubbly chin of a tall male.

'Well, good morning, Sis!' The voice sounded very Australian, which of course was no surprise.

Involuntarily she took a step back and stared up into the man's laughing blue eyes. Curly brown hair hung over his forehead. His grin showed beautiful white teeth. One of Uncle John's sons—must have arrived last night, after she had gone to bed. He was deeply tanned all over. Kristin could see almost all of his marvellous physique, for all he wore was a pair of bright blue undershorts with an orange sun blazing on the front.

'Good morning,' she mumbled feebly.

'Kristin, I presume? I'm Scott.' He extended his hand. 'I'm pleased to finally meet you, Kristin.'

She felt utterly ridiculous standing there shaking hands with a stranger in undershorts.

'Nice to meet you too,' she said awkwardly, aware that his eyes were sliding over her in bold appraisal. Uncombed, unwashed, and still half asleep, she was less than delighted.

He let go of her hand and gestured in the direction of the bathroom. 'Ladies first.'

Gratefully she slipped through the door and closed it, expelling a long breath. Why was she always so uneasy in awkward situations? Some people seemed to have a knack for passing over embarrassment with some bright and funny comment. Why couldn't she be cool and come up with a clever line rather than stand there like a gawky schoolgirl? Her reflection in the mirror made her groan. She looked sixteen, not twenty-two.

By the time she had showered, washed and dried her hair, then put on make-up and clothes, she felt and looked her age. Her face looked pale because of the lack of tan and she rubbed in a little extra blusher as she scrutinised herself in the mirror in her room.

She had put on green shorts and a green-and-white striped top, and it felt strange wearing them in December after she had been wearing jeans and sweaters for the last few months. Her legs looked white—yuk! She rummaged through her cosmetics bag and found a bottle of nail polish. She painted her toenails a dark pink, but her legs didn't look any less pale.

She contemplated her hair. Leave it loose or tie it back? She left it loose. It had been trimmed a few weeks earlier and it hung down to her shoulders, not really straight and not really curly. It was a warm brown with some reddish highlights, nothing very exciting, but it seemed to suit her best. As a teenager she had experimented with different hair colours, bleaching it blonde and dyeing it red, both of which had been disastrous. Now she left well enough alone. Not everybody could be a flaming redhead or a sexy blonde.

People like her were destined to be more average—grey eyes, brown hair, not terribly extroverted and not particularly brilliant in school.

Oh, well, she thought philosophically, if ever a man marries me it won't be for my beauty or my money. There was comfort in that thought.

The kitchen was bright and sunny and the fragrance of freshly brewed coffee permeated the air. Scott, shaven and dressed, was sitting at the table eating fried eggs and toast and her mother was emptying the dishwasher.

'Your mother,' said Scott, 'makes the best fried eggs in the world.'

'She's had a little practice,' Kristin returned, which was an understatement of some magnitude. Running a small-town restaurant had given her plenty of experience in preparing eggs to the detailed specifications of a multitude of fussy customers. Pouring herself a cup of coffee, Kristin sat down across from Scott, who observed her with interest.

'Are you the same girl I just met upstairs in the hall? You looked about fifteen.'

'That bad?' she smiled. 'I was still half asleep.' She stirred the sugar into her coffee and added milk, studying Scott surreptitiously. He was certainly one of the more handsome men she had come across lately. He was sportily dressed in shorts, a T-shirt and cheap thongs, apparently planning a leisurely day.

'You want some eggs, Kristin?' asked her mother.

'Just toast and coffee. I had too much to eat on the plane yesterday. They kept feeding us and I kept eating.'

Scott made a face. 'Revolting stuff!'

'It wasn't bad. Besides, I'm used to eating in the school cafeteria, and after that anything tastes good.' She buttered a piece of toast, glancing up to see her mother still busy putting dishes away. 'Come sit with us, Mom.'

'I will—just a minute.'

Scott pushed a jar of jam across the table. 'Try this. Mango jam—your mother made it.'

'*Mango* jam?' She picked up the jar, peeped into it and sniffed it. It smelled sweet and fruity.

Amused, he watched her. 'Something wrong with that?'

'It smells wonderful, but I've never had mango jam, or mangoes, for that matter.'

'You'll have plenty of 'em here.' He waved his hand at the yard visible through the window, a luscious green shining in the splendour of the summer sun. 'We've got a couple of trees in the garden.'

Kristin spread the jam on the toast and took a bite. 'It's delicious!'

'Of course it is—your mother made it. I tell you, since my father married her I've been sorely tempted to move back home.'

'You're a terrible charmer, Scott,' said Kristin's mother as she took a seat next to him.

He grinned, put his arm around her and kissed her on the cheek. 'Too bad I'm not fifteen years older—I'd steal you away from Dad! I don't suppose you go for younger men, do you?' He looked at her hopefully.

'Only rich ones.'

'Well, that leaves me out.' He sighed. 'I knew there was a good reason not to give up banking.'

Kristin loved listening to his accent, and he accommodated her by talking a lot. He had driven all the way down the coast from Arrawarra to Sydney to meet her. Eight hours of driving just to meet her, he said, and she was in bed when he finally arrived at his father's house at ten last night. He gave her an accusing look.

'I didn't know you were coming.' Ridiculously, she almost felt guilty.

His face broke in a boyish grin. 'Neither did I, actually, until the last moment. I'm running a caravan park together with a mate and it's a hectic time of year just now.'

'A caravan park?'

'A camp ground,' her mother explained. 'A caravan is a camper.' She poured them all another cup of coffee.

Scott shook his head. 'You Americans don't even understand plain English.' He sighed again. 'Anyway, running this place wasn't exactly what I thought it might be, but it's an education.'

Until six months ago he had worked for the Australia–New Zealand Bank in Sydney. In spite of the casual attire he was wearing now, Kristin could easily imagine him there with his clean good looks—one of those conspicuous Bright Young Men sporting designer shirts, Gucci shoes, Piaget watches and expensive haircuts, climbing the ladder of success.

The world of high finance, however, was not for Scott. Life simply could not be taken that seriously. He had wanted out, so he departed. Together with an adventurous friend he managed to buy a piece of beach property and converted it into a caravan park. And now, knee-deep in complaining vacationers, broken washers and blaring radios, he was wondering if this was what he really wanted. He had imagined himself lazing on the beach and birdwatching in the early morning hours, but instead he had to deal with garbage collection (rubbish, he called it), repair men, customer complaints and dogs that had been secretly smuggled into the park by their owners.

For an hour he kept both of them laughing with his stories.

He had decided, he said, that since Kristin was only here for a few short weeks, he would take it upon himself to show her Sydney, a task he seemed not at all reluctant to perform. She smiled and said, yes, she'd like that, and he looked pleased.

There were only a few days left before Christmas and there was plenty to do around the house. That afternoon Kristin made a batch of eggnog, a concoction the Australians apparently were not familiar with. Straddling a kitchen chair, Scott watched her with mock suspicion as she whipped up egg whites and cream and mixed in milk, but his face brightened when she added rum and whisky. He reached for a glass and held it out to her.

Kristin shook her head. 'You can't have any yet. It has to sit for a while so the flavours can blend and mellow.'

The disappointment in his face would have melted a gangster's heart. 'Surely I can have a taste now?'

She smiled at him cheerfully. 'Absolutely not! Christmas Eve, not before. And according to the recipe that's not even long enough. We should leave it at least a week.'

'I thought in America everything was instant.'

'Not the good things in life.'

'Such as eggnog?'

'Such as *homemade* eggnog. You can buy cartons of a non-alcoholic base in the supermarket and add rum to it at home, but it's not nearly as good as the real stuff. You just wait and be patient.'

He sighed and marched out the kitchen. 'I'll wait in the lounge.'

'Lounge? Oh, you mean living room.'

'No! I mean *lounge*!' he yelled over his shoulder.

Laughing, Kristin began to rinse out the mixing bowl.

The next morning she helped her mother do some baking—cranberry bread and date-and-nut bread and chewy Noels and Christmas stars. The house was full of delicious aromas, and even though outside the world was green and blooming, inside it began to feel and smell like Christmas. A big decorated Christmas tree stood in the corner of the living room, bright with lights and tinsel and shiny ornaments.

In the afternoon Scott offered to do the last major pre-holiday grocery shopping, and Kristin went with him. They parked in a gigantic parking lot, just like the ones at home, and entered the big air-conditioned building. Scott examined the long list and whistled.

'We may need more than one trolley for this lot,' he said with a grin.

'Trolley?'

He rolled his eyes heavenward. 'Don't tell me you have a different word for that too!'

'Of course. A trolley is something you transport people in, not cheese! A trolley is a tram, a streetcar— you know, like they have in San Francisco.'

'I hope you'll excuse me for not having been to San Francisco,' he said with mock sarcasm. 'So tell me, what *do* you call this contraption in the United States of America?'

'A shopping cart, what else?'

'Trolley would be good.'

'Shopping cart makes more sense. It's more descriptive.'

He narrowed his eyes. 'I'm not going to fight with a foreigner.' He marched off down the aisle in dignified silence.

Kristin added *trolley* to the Australian–American dictionary she was compiling mentally. *Bench*—counter. *Caravan*—camper. *Garden*—yard. *Holiday*—vacation. *Lounge*—living room. *Mate*—buddy. *Postman*— mailman, letter carrier (the new, non-sexist word). *Rubbish*—garbage. *Serviette*—napkin. *Teatowel*— dishtowel. *Trolley*—shopping cart.

She examined the store. It looked in no way different from a supermarket at home. Even many of the products and brands were the same. The fruit and vegetables looked wonderful, especially because in her mind she still equated December with winter.

'You like rock melon?' asked Scott, checking the list.

'I don't know—I've never had any.'

'You must grow them in America!'

She shrugged. 'I don't know. What's a rock melon?'

'This.' He picked up a cantaloupe.

Kristin laughed. 'Oh, of course we have those. It's a. . . .'

'*Rock melon*,' he supplied with dire threat in his voice.

'Cantaloupe, you mean.'

He glared at her. 'I don't want to hear about it. You people are defiling the English language.'

'Hah! You don't sound exactly as if you grew up in mother England, either! You people came a lot further than we did!'

He was easy to be with, easy to talk to and joke with. She felt comfortable with him as she had felt comfortable with Rick. Scott reminded her of him a little—the same easy-going type. She felt her throat thicken at the thought of Rick and she swallowed hastily. For three years he had been her friend. It would take a while before she would be used to the idea of his death. And again she felt the pinprick of fear.

After Uncle John came home from work that night, Scott started the barbecue. 'Chops for dinner tonight,' he stated, making quite a production out of lighting the charcoal.

Kristin made the salad, using lettuce and vegetables straight from the vegetable garden. She wondered how she could possibly adjust again to winter in a few weeks. Spring and summer were glorious in Oregon, but still so far away.

While they waited for the chops to cook, she strolled around the garden with Uncle John, who pointed out the various trees and shrubs. There were tall banana plants, two mango trees, a tangelo tree and a blooming jacaranda, which had flowered for the second time that year because of some quirk in the weather. He loved his garden and told her he spent every weekend and most of his evenings working in it. It looked beautiful—such a lovely peaceful place. No wonder her mother was happy here after all those years of lonely struggle.

It all seemed so unreal, even now. Not many foreigners came to the small coastal town in Oregon where her mother had run a small seaside restaurant. But John Baldwin had wandered into the place one evening, had slipped on some unknown substance and gone sprawling between the tables, breaking a leg in the process. Horrified, her mother had handled the situation as well as possible, calling an ambulance, visiting the hospital afterwards, doing whatever she could to make Mr John Baldwin as comfortable as possible so far away from home. Strangely, he had not departed for Australia as soon as the doctor gave him the okay to travel, but stayed around in a nearby motel. Her mother worried about a lawsuit. Six weeks later it wasn't a lawsuit she got but a marriage proposal.

Home for a weekend from college, Kristin had been stunned at the difference in her mother. She was practically blooming with love and looked ten years younger. Kristin could understand why. Not only was John Baldwin tall and handsome, but he was warm and loving to boot. Warmth and love were things Kristin's mother hadn't had much of, having been widowed at an early age.

It hadn't been easy for Kristin to see the house and restaurant sold. She had lived in the house all her life and she had worked in the restaurant every vacation since she had been old enough. It was even harder to see her mother leave to go so far away.

The chops turned out to be lamb and not pork as Kristin had assumed. She had had lamb only on rare occasions at home and she enjoyed the meal, listening to Scott and his father discuss the news of the day.

During the next few days, Scott marched her all over Sydney to show her the sights. They toured the harbour, and she loved the feel of the wind in her hair and the sun on her face. Blue-green water glittered in the sun. Sailboats, white or brightly coloured, gallivanted all over the harbour, and on the banks red roofs peaked between the lush greenery of trees and bushes. Scott stood next to her on the railing of the tour boat, looking down into her face with laughing eyes.

'You're enjoying it, aren't you? The most beautiful harbour in the world, they say.'

'I haven't been around the world, but it's surely the most beautiful one I've ever seen.' She smiled at him. 'I wish I knew how to thank you. I'm having the time of my life, you know.'

His smile deepened. His arm came around her shoulder and his eyes were sparkling with laughter as he bent his face closer to hers. 'No thanks necessary. It's a joy to take you around,' he said softly. Kristin didn't move as his mouth touched hers and lingered there in a sensuous caress. When he straightened away, she looked out over the water, avoiding his eyes.

They had a Yum Cha lunch at Shanghai Village in Chinatown, and one night they ate paella at Doyles in Watson's Bay, drinking wine they had brought themselves. Apparently, bringing your own bottle was an accepted custom. The restaurant supplied the glasses.

Sitting outside on the terrace, they had a view of the bay. They watched the sunset as they ate paella thick with crab and prawns and fish and mussels. The sky was streaked orange and pink and lavender as the sun slowly sank behind the horizon. A few small boats were out on the water and the picture was one of serenity and peace as the colours slowly faded into dusky greys and purples.

One night Scott took her to the Marble Bar that had once been part of the old Adams Hotel which had been torn down. The bar had been reconstructed and on top of it now towered the Hilton Hotel. The bar décor was a Victorian delight with its stained glass windows, brass railings, marble table tops, carved wood and romantic paintings of women and children on the walls. They were lucky to find a place and they sat down with a drink to watch the band, all dressed in black. New Orleans jazz vibrated through the place and a few couples were gyrating enthusiastically to the music.

Sipping her drink, Kristin watched. A bald man with a beer belly and a windbreaker was dancing himself into a frenzy with a buxomy blonde in a wrinkled red dress.

She hadn't felt so lighthearted in a long time. The pressure of exams was over. For the last two months she had worked very hard, and with her part-time job at the university library taking up most of her spare time there never seemed much opportunity for fun and games. She realised now how much she needed a change of pace.

One night they had a simple meal at a corner café at Kings Cross and afterwards strolled around to see the sights. Coffee shops and massage parlours and exclusive restaurants and strip joints and porno movies and jewellery shops all mingled peacefully together. Music and lights and laughter spilled out into the street. People everywhere—tourists and artists and vacant-looking teenage girls with short skirts and lots of make-up lounging against doorposts. The sadness hidden behind those empty-looking faces was in sharp contrast with the cheer and colour all around them.

They strolled around leisurely, Scott's arm casually around her shoulders, and she took everything in and listened to Scott, who seemed to have a never-ending supply of stories and jokes.

She fell in love with Sydney, beautiful and clean and cosmopolitan and sophisticated with its fancy restaurants and hotels, its Chinatown, its beaches and beautiful harbour. The famous Opera House was the most magnificent building she had ever seen.

On Christmas Eve they stayed at home and Kristin helped her mother with the preparations for the next day's dinner. It was obvious how much her mother enjoyed doing this for a family, her own now, having so many times spent Christmas at the house of relatives.

She was looking forward to meeting Paul. He lived on the other side of Sydney, but had been in Western Australia for the past few weeks and would not be home until today.

They were sitting outside drinking coffee when they heard his car come up the driveway. Moments later a man rounded the corner of the house. He was big and broad-shouldered, taller than Scott and a few years older. He had dark, short-cropped hair, bright blue eyes, a square chin and rugged features. The left side of his face had had an unlucky meeting with something hard and sharp. A long scar ran across his cheek from chin to temple. He wasn't handsome by any stretch of the imagination, but it was an arresting face, not one you would forget easily.

Having greeted the others, he turned to Kristin, regarding her with calm interest as he extended his hand.

'Hello, Kristin.'

She put her hand in his and looked into the vivid blue eyes under heavy dark brows. A curious sensation curled in her stomach. His handshake was firm. Her face grew warm as his gaze lingered on, and then he smiled and his eyes crinkled at the corners.

'I've been looking forward to meeting you,' he said, his voice deep and vibrant, and her heart made a ridiculous somersault. She didn't know why she reacted like that, but the very size of the man overwhelmed her.

He let go of her hand and turned his gaze back to the others, and involuntarily Kristin let out a sigh, aware suddenly of the rapid beating of her heart.

It was the strangest evening of her life. She was very quiet, listening to the others talk. Her eyes kept moving back to Paul without conscious thought and every now and then she would catch him looking at her. When

dark came they went inside, and Kristin brought out
the eggnog and filled the glasses.

Paul sat across from her, limbs loose and relaxed,
slowly sipping the creamy mixture as he observed her
over the rim of his glass. She felt unaccountably
nervous. His eyes were narrowed slightly and a faint
smile tugged at the corners of his mouth. She wondered
why he was looking at her like that and what he was
thinking.

It took her a long time to fall asleep that night, and
when she finally did, she dreamed of the brilliant blue
eyes following her everywhere.

CHAPTER TWO

IT was the loveliest Christmas she had ever had, even without cold and snow. Sunshine streamed through the open windows and birds chirped cheerfully in the bushes as they sat in the lounge and opened their packages. They were laughing and talking, drinking coffee and eating hot raisin muffins straight from the oven. Kristin looked around the room, seeing all the happy faces—her mother, Uncle John, Paul and Scott, feeling a rush of sentimentality. *They are my family now!* she thought with a leap of her heart. And it was then for the first time that she felt a surge of regret at having to go back to the States. But go back she had to. She had to finish college and graduate in June.

The prospect of being alone had never seemed worse. She wanted to stay here with these people who gave her their friendship and love and acceptance freely.

She shifted in the chair. Good lord, she was going all mushy and schmaltzy! She took a deep breath. All she needed now was to get weepy and have everyone think she was a complete fool.

The turkey dinner, complete with stuffing and cranberry sauce and pumpkin pie for dessert, was delicious. Kristin ate more than she normally did as she quietly listened to Scott telling jokes and Paul giving an account of the opening of his exhibition in a gallery in Perth, while her mother and Uncle John just sat there looking happy.

It all seemed too much, too good to be true. She felt a shiver of apprehension.

They talked until late, sitting on the terrace in the warm night air. Finally Uncle John called it a day, reached for his wife's hand and took off for bed.

Yawning elaborately, Scott followed them into the house.

'How about if we finish the last of the eggnog?' asked Paul, coming to his feet. He towered over her, smiling down at her in the dark.

'That'd be nice.' Oh, why couldn't she think of something bright to say?'

He came back with two glasses, not quite full. 'This has been the nicest Christmas I've had in years,' he commented as he settled his tall frame back in the chair.

'For me too,' Kristin answered.

'Your mother is a lovely person.'

'Thank you.' She hesitated. 'You and Scott don't seem to mind at all that your father married again,' she ventured.

'I did, actually, I told him if he married again I'd cut him out of my will.' She stared at him and he laughed out loud. 'Why should we mind? Your mother is wonderful and she's made him happy.'

She nodded thoughtfully. 'It's just that you hear so often of resentments and objections when parents get married again.'

Paul shrugged lightly. 'Scott and I are both grown up and we don't live at home. My mother died eight years ago and I'm glad to see my father happy again. Being alone is no good if you're not used to it.'

Her eyes met his briefly, then moved away. 'No. My mother was alone for nineteen years. My father died when I was only three.'

'How long did she run that restaurant?'

'For all that time. She took over from my father. It was only a small place, but she was always working, and in the vacations I would help out. It wasn't an easy life for her.'

'And for you?'

She looked up, surprised. 'For me? Oh, it wasn't so bad. I was alone a lot. The house was right behind the restaurant and I'd go in now and then to talk to my mother. I always knew where to find her if I needed her. Weekends and holidays weren't so nice because we were open most of the time. She had some help, of course, but the responsibility was all hers. It's good to see her have it a little easier now.'

'You don't resent her leaving you?'

'I'm in college. I was only home once a month or so. But it's a lonely feeling knowing I can't even do that now. It's a strange idea that the restaurant doesn't belong to us any more and that someone else lives in our house. I grew up there. It's the only place I've ever called home.' She shrugged and smiled. 'But I should be able to stand on my own two feet, shouldn't I? I'll graduate this June and I know I wouldn't ever live at home any more anyway. It's just a funny feeling not to have a place to go home to.'

'I suppose Australia is too far to count,' he admitted.

'I wish it weren't—you're all so nice. I really feel welcome here.'

'And you are, of course.' There was a smile in his voice.

'Thank you.'

He laughed softly. 'You sound so formal!'

'I suppose so.' Kristin laughed as well, then looked around the yard with its exotic fruit trees, hearing the strange sounds of the night creatures, so different from home, so far away. 'When I was a child,' she said slowly, 'I never thought things would change. I didn't think I'd ever leave my own small town. I thought my mother and I would live in the same house for ever, run the restaurant for ever. And now ... everything is changing.'

'Does it frighten you?' Paul's voice was soft in the quiet night, odd coming from this big bulk of a man.

His question surprised her a little, for it was exactly how she felt and he had sensed it. 'I suppose what scares me,' she said thoughtfully, 'is not so much the new, but losing the old and familiar. Like losing your security blanket when you're little.'

They talked. She told him about her life in the small coastal town of Oregon, about the redwood tree house a kindly neighbour had built for her. He had been like a substitute grandfather to her, and she had called him Grandpa Jones. She could still see him sitting in his rocking chair on his weathered porch, smoking a pipe. Two fingers on his right hand were missing, lopped off in an accident at the lumber mill where he had worked all his life.

Kristin had spent endless hours in the tree house with her cat in her lap, doing homework or reading, crunching shiny red apples. She had worked her way through stacks of books from the school library—*Mark Twain and Huckleberry Finn*, *The Secret Garden*, *Alice in Wonderland*, *Heidi*, *Treasure Island*, and countless others.

What would happen to the tree house now? It had still been there when the restaurant and house were sold. Maybe it would be broken down, or other children would play in it. She had always thought that one day her own children would play in it. Maybe, one day, she would go back and find out.

The night was full of sounds and the air felt velvety soft. A breeze rustled the trees. She was conscious of Paul's eyes all the time, blue eyes that kept scanning her face and made her a little uneasy, but excited too in a strange, breathless way. She felt a sense of exhilaration, a heightening of the senses. Never before had she been so physically aware of a man, felt such an alarming attraction. It was there between them, the electricity, that strange state of tension—evident in the words and the gestures and the smiles. It was an extraordinary experience to feel such instant, intense affinity with another person.

'You're not at all what you'd expect a typical American girl to be,' he said suddenly, and she looked at him in surprise.

'What's your idea of a typical American girl? I always

thought we came in a variety of types, sizes and colours.'

He laughed. 'Of course. But I always think of them as being rather outgoing, extroverted, a bit aggressive and everything up front.' He studied her thoughtfully for a moment. 'You're not like that. I think you're normally very quiet. I don't think you talk to many people the way you talked to me tonight.'

He was right, of course, and it was unnerving to know how well he had gauged her. She twirled her empty glass, not looking at him. She wished she could think of something to say.

'Am I embarrassing you?' he asked.

When she glanced up she saw the amusement in his face, and grinned selfconsciously. 'I guess you're right. I've been talking quite a lot tonight. Usually I have trouble talking to people. When I first went to college I had a terrible time—all those new faces! And everybody seemed to know how, what, and where, and I felt so lost. All I wanted was to run back home. The high school in my town was very small and everyone knew everyone else and. . . .' She stopped abruptly. 'Oh, my, there I go again!' She grinned apologetically.

'Never mind. Go on.'

Hesitating, she moved a mushroom around the plate with her fork. 'I wasn't used to all that anonymity. It was awful. I had a hard time making friends. I didn't know how to start a conversation with a stranger and nobody seemed to notice me. I felt invisible, like a small grey mouse sitting in a corner.'

'So you hid behind your books and sat in your room every night and studied.'

She shrugged. 'I didn't know what else to do.'

Things hadn't changed until one day Rick had sat down at her table in the cafeteria, which was packed full with lunchtime eaters. He had started talking to her as if he had known her all his life, complaining first about the food, then about one of his instructors.

He had warm brown eyes, big feet, and a spicy vocabulary, and within ten minutes he had her choking with laughter. He ended up pounding her back, not very delicately, when her milk went down the wrong way. She watched him go back for more dessert for both of them, seeing the lanky body wind itself through the throng of students with ease and athletic grace. His jeans were old and faded and his T-shirt displayed some expression in Spanish with exclamation marks in front and back.

After they had finished their dessert, he walked her to her next class (history, she still remembered it), which happened to be in the same building as his. After class he was waiting for her and asked her to come to a party with him the next evening. Much later he told her he had thought she looked like such a sad little mouse that he had felt sorry for her.

'It took a while before I made friends, but after that it was easier,' she said to Paul. There was the sound of flapping wings out in the dark of the yard—fruit bats flying around the banana plants. The moon was almost full, and the sky was bright with stars. A romantic night, she thought, and felt a sudden rush of warmth when Paul's hand touched hers.

'I'd like to take some photographs of you,' he said unexpectedly. 'Will you let me?'

She was stunned. 'Of me? Why?'

He laughed. 'Why do you think? I like your face, your eyes, your mouth. There's a lot of expression in it.'

'Oh, I. . . .' Kristin swallowed, surprised. 'I guess so. Did you bring your camera?'

'I never leave home without them.'

They—plural. Of course, a professional photographer wouldn't have merely one like ordinary souls. He probably had a collection. He liked her face. That was why he had been looking at her so much, evaluating her as a subject. She should be pleased, shouldn't she? Why then did she feel disappointed? She disengaged her hand and leaned back in her chair.

'What's the matter?' he asked.

'Nothing.' He had read her expression, of course. He had done nothing but study her face since he had arrived last night. He would notice everything in it. She felt suddenly exposed and vulnerable, as if she didn't even have the privacy of her own feelings and thoughts. She felt foolish for having talked to him so freely about herself.

Rising to her feet, she put on a smile. 'I'm tired, I think I'll go to bed now. Goodnight, Paul.' But before she had taken one step he pulled her down next to him.

'If you don't want me to photograph you, just say so. It won't hurt my feelings for more than a year or so.'

She couldn't help smiling then. 'It's all right, I don't mind,' she said awkwardly. 'I just don't know what to do.'

'Just leave it to me. Don't worry about it. Tomorrow then, okay?'

He let go of her hand and she got up and walked into the house, faint disappointment still with her.

The photographic session was a disaster. Whatever Paul wanted her to do or not do, Kristin wasn't sure. She only knew she wasn't in the best of moods, and she supposed it showed, somehow, to the all-seeing Paul Baldwin.

They were outside in sun-dappled shade, all his gear parked on the picnic table and a camera perched on a tripod. For the past half hour he had been ordering her around in short, clipped sentences, and his frustration was obvious. Whatever it was he wanted, he wasn't getting. It made her increasingly nervous; it was probably her fault. Still, her anger grew by the minute at his curtness, and when his irritation came blasting out in his raised voice once more, she jumped up to her feet and ran inside on shaking legs.

To hell with him and his damned pictures! She didn't

need it. Rushing into her bedroom, she closed the door
and sank down on her bed, fighting back tears.

Knocking on her door. 'Kristin?'

'Go away! I'm through! I quit!'

Paul strode right in. 'I want a word with you.'

Kristin jerked upright. The audacity! 'Get out of my
room!'

'When I'm finished.' His voice held no compromise.
He moved his feet apart a little and jammed his hands
in his jeans pockets. 'Now what was the matter with
you today? If you didn't want to sit for me, why didn't
you tell me? I couldn't do a thing with your face. You
looked as if you hated every minute of it.'

She refused to answer. It took all her strength not to
burst into tears. She hated herself for feeling so
inadequate, for not being able to handle the situation
with a little more grace and a little less emotion.

When she maintained a dogged silence, Paul turned
on his heel, marched out of the room and closed the
door quietly behind him.

The tears came then and she buried her face in the
pillow and wept. What's the matter with me? she
thought miserably. *What is the matter with me?* This
wasn't like her, acting like a spoiled brat and being so
emotional over nothing.

Later that afternoon she went downstairs and found
everyone outside around the picnic table which now
held the tea things. Her mother was definitely getting
Australianised, serving tea in the afternoon! There was
no sign of any of Paul's equipment, but Paul himself
was sitting at the table, stirring his tea. He looked
steadily at Kristin as she approached them, but she
refused to meet his eyes and sat down without a word.

From the colourful plate of biscuits and cake she
selected a piece of cranberry bread and ate it slowly. To
her relief no one seemed to notice anything amiss,
although she could feel the tension quivering between
Paul and herself. Tea finally over, she offered to clear

the table. She gathered things on a tray and carried them into the kitchen. Paul followed her in. She sensed him standing behind her and her nerves grew taut.

'Kristin?'

'Yes?' She turned on the tap without looking at him and began to rinse out the teapot.

'Will you look at me, please?'

She turned, forcing her eyes to meet his, saying nothing.

'I apologise for losing my temper.' His voice was composed, his eyes calm. 'I don't seem to have the best control when I'm working.'

Kristin swallowed. 'I'm sorry I was no good.'

'Something was bothering you, I could tell. I knew what I wanted—what I wanted to capture in your face, but it wasn't there any more. I'd been watching you all Christmas Day and it was there, and today it was gone. It was frustrating, but I shouldn't have become angry. I'm sorry.'

'It's all right, forget it.' What else was there to say? She felt awkward standing there with a dripping teapot in her hand.

There was a brief silence.

'Scott told me he's been doing the town with you,' Paul commented at last, changing the subject.

'Yes. It was very nice. He's a good guide.'

'I'm sure.' There was faint mockery in his tone, but his eyes were amused. 'Did he take you to the Summit, by any chance?'

'The Summit? No. What is it?'

'A revolving restaurant on top of a very high building. The best view of Sydney you'll ever have, and all while you're eating superb food. Would you like to go?'

It sounded wonderful, but she hesitated with her answer.

'What's the matter? Don't you want to go?'

'Oh, yes! But—well, you know, you don't have to feel obliged.'

Paul laughed. 'I do not feel obliged—I'm asking because I want to. Simple.'

'I'd like to very much,' she said gravely, attempting a smile and hoping she was pulling it off with a little grace.

'Tomorrow night all right?'

She nodded. 'Thank you.'

Scott sauntered into the kitchen, chewing on a blade of grass. 'I have this fantastic idea—brilliant, actually.' He smiled radiantly. 'Kristin, when I go back to Arrawarra tomorrow, why don't you go with me? Beach, sunshine, swimming—you'll love it!'

'She can't leave tomorrow,' said Paul before Kristin could say a word. 'She's going out with me in the evening.'

Scott, hands on his hips, looked at his brother with narrowed eyes. 'I don't know if I like that, mate. You'd better behave yourself. Remember, I had her first.'

Paul grinned. 'Well, perhaps we'll have to duel over her—ten paces with wet tea-towels?'

Scott gave him a withering look, then turned to Kristin, reproach in his eyes. 'I'm disappointed in you. One week, and you're unfaithful already! But I'll forgive you as long as you promise you'll go with me to Arrawarra. I'll wait for you; one more day isn't going to make a difference, I suppose. How about it?'

Kristin hesitated. She loved camping and swimming and lazing on the beach, but she had arrived only a week ago and it didn't seem right to leave her mother again so soon.

'I just got here,' she said uncertainly, just as her mother entered the kitchen.

'What's this about?' she asked.

'Scott's invited me to come along with him to Arrawarra,' explained Kristin.

'Why don't you do that? We'll all be up there later in the week, anyway, for New Year's Eve. This way you'll get a few extra days.' Her mother looked at Paul. 'You're coming too, aren't you?'

He nodded, smiling. He had been silently watching the exchange, arms crossed over his chest. 'Wouldn't miss the festivities for the world.'

'On New Year's Eve the park is going to organise a big barbecue for all the campers,' said Scott, leaning a lazy hip against the counter. 'We'll roast a whole pig and a lamb and we'll have fireworks on the beach.'

Kristin gave in. 'It sounds wonderful. The beach in December—I can't quite imagine it.' She looked down on her bare legs. 'I could use some colour, that's for sure.'

Eyes glinting triumphantly, Scott punched his brother playfully on the shoulder. 'Hah! I've got her for the rest of the week, mate! Don't understand what she sees in your ugly face anyway.'

Kristin's eyes flashed to Paul's face, but he seemed not at all disturbed by his brother's words. She wondered why he hadn't done anything about that scar on his face. Certainly plastic surgery should improve the appearance of it considerably.

Paul observed his brother with calm superiority. 'And you, baby-face,' he said soberly, 'had better watch out. At the rate you're consuming females you'll be worn out by the time you're thirty!'

'You two stop bickering!' Kristin's mother scolded, as if talking to two little boys. 'And one of you take these milk bottles and put them near the mail box.'

Scott grinned broadly as he took the caddy from her. 'Letter box,' he corrected.

She glared at him. 'Watch out, sonny!' she threatened, and Scott ambled out the back door, laughing.

Through the kitchen window Kristin watched him stroll down the driveway, hearing the clanging of the bottles and seeing the bobbing of the inverted plastic cups on top of the bottles. Early in the morning the milkman would pick up the empty bottles and replace them with full ones, covering them with the plastic glasses to prevent the birds from picking open the foil seals and drinking the milk. Suburban gardens were populated with the most audacious birds. Uncle John had pointed them out to her on various occasions—the kookaburra, the kurrawong with its bright yellow eyes and loud call, and the miner birds, loud and aggressive, fighting for territory by chasing other birds away.

The next evening Kristin stood in front of her closet and stared in desperation at her clothes. She hadn't come prepared for fancy outings. The only good dress she had brought was the peacock-blue one which she had worn on Christmas Day. Well, there wasn't anything she could do about it—she'd have to wear it again. Briefly she considered asking someone to take her to Chatswood Chase to try and find something else in one of the stores there, then shelved the idea. It made little sense to spend money on a dress she probably wouldn't wear again for months. At school all you saw were jeans and more jeans. Money wasn't something she could afford to waste.

She wished that for once she didn't have to be practical. That she could just go out and buy the sexiest, slinkiest dress in town. She wished she didn't always have to think about money. There had never been much, never enough for real splurges, real extravagances. In the bank at home she now had some money from the sale of the restaurant—her share, according to her mother, for her help over the years. But that money she couldn't touch, wouldn't touch. One day she might need it—really need it. And again there was the faint fear in the background, and she quickly suppressed it.

She wished she was beautiful and brilliant and sparkling—someone a man might enjoy. The thought of being alone with Paul for an entire evening was unnerving. He would get bored with her. What would she talk about? A man like him would need more stimulating company than she knew how to be.

His car was comfortable but modest. Soft music issued from the stereo. She leaned back and tried to relax. It was ridiculous to be so nervous. She gazed out of the window, hoping he wouldn't notice. The scenery sped by—beautiful suburbs with lots of greenery. Paul talked calmly, asking her a question now and then, and soon she felt herself loosen up. When they arrived in the city, he parked the car and they walked to a tall circular building.

'Australia Square,' announced Paul.

'It's *round*!'

'Someone got confused,' he grinned. 'Anyway, the restaurant is on the top, the forty-seventh floor.'

Kristin looked up at the expansive mass of steel and concrete. 'I hope the elevator doesn't get stuck halfway,' she said drily.

'The lift? I doubt it.' He smiled, sparks of humour in his eyes. 'Do you know the joke about the Englishman and the American waiting for a lift?'

She shook her head. 'No.'

They entered the building, found the bank of elevators, and Paul pushed the top button. 'All right, let me see. The Englishman and the American were waiting for the lift. "I've been waiting for the lift for five minutes now," complained the Englishman. "Elevator, you mean," said the American. "Certainly not," countered the Englishman. *"Lift."* The American grinned. "Hate to tell you this, buddy," he said, "but *we* invented the thing." The Englishman gave him a haughty look. "And *we*, sir, invented the *language*."'

Kristin laughed. 'I like it! I'll have to try and remember that one.'

The lift had arrived. The doors swished open, then closed behind them. They zoomed to the top floor at breathtaking speed. Seconds later they stepped out into the green interior of the restaurant—subdued lighting,

soft piano music, waiters in evening dress. The room
was circular and they sat near the window. The view
was spectacular, slowly changing as the restaurant floor
revolved.

'This is fantastic,' Kristin whispered as she watched
the scene below stretching out for miles around. The
low sun shone on downtown Sydney and slowly the
Hilton Hotel and the American Express building
floated by, or such was the impression. 'How fast are
we moving?'

'It's on the menu, here. Four feet a minute. It takes an
hour and forty-five minutes to go all the way around.'

A waiter in black appeared to take their order. He
looked like someone from an old English novel, formal
and serious and dignified, as if en route to the theatre.

'What will you have to drink?' asked Paul.

Kristin gave him a helpless look, not sure what to
order. In college her drinking had limited itself to beer
and cheap California wine, neither of which seemed
appropriate. She wondered what would happen if she
asked for a glass of Gallo wine. The waiter would
probably faint—that was, if he knew what she was
talking about.

'Any suggestions?' she asked. 'I'm not used to having
before-dinner drinks. Hamburgers and pizzas don't
require them.'

'How about a Golden Dream? Suits you just right.
It's sweet.' He was laughing at her with his eyes. 'It has
orange juice, cream, Cointreau and Galliano in it.'

'Sounds sinful! I'll try it.'

It was delicious—sweet and fruity and creamy and
quite potent. Kristin could feel herself relax.

'Decadent stuff,' she said, and Paul grinned.

'This is a decadent night. Wait till you taste the food!'

They started with oyster au naturel, which seemed to
Kristin a fancy name for oysters on the half shell. Being
a true Oregonian she loved seafood of any kind and it
was an easy subject to talk about.

Tonight was one of those times when she would have given her eye-teeth to be more sophisticated, a better conversationalist, more confident. And more than that, she wanted to be beautiful and sexy. She realised with a sudden skipping of her heart that she wanted Paul to look at her with admiration and desire in his eyes. She gazed at the deep pink carnation on the table as she chewed another oyster. Would she ever learn to be sophisticated? If she hadn't learned by now, at the age of twenty-two, she probably wouldn't.

With Rick she had felt at ease, as she did with Scott. They were the playful, easy-going types, full of boyish charm. They didn't seem to take life too seriously, didn't seem to judge people, but accepted them for what they were. Rick had never criticised her seriously, never made her feel lacking in anything. He would tease her lightly, as Scott teased her, but she had never felt he was critical of her.

She did not exactly feel that Paul was critical of her— at least not, in any negative sense. Still, she was always aware of his eyes, the assessment in them, the observation of her, of her actions and her words. It made her nervous.

The oysters were finished. She raised her eyes to his. 'You're always looking at me,' she said impulsively.

He smiled at her. 'It's my profession—looking, watching, seeing. Once you learn how to see, the world is full of wonders.' He was speaking in a quiet tone and the words settled in her mind. Did he think she was one of those wonders? Good lord, he must have terrific eyes!

'How did you get started in photography?' she asked, and saw him grimace at the memory. His first camera had been given to him by his grandfather for his twelfth birthday, he told her, and by the time he was sixteen photography had become almost an obsession. He had set up a darkroom for developing and printing his films. All his allowance went into photographic equipment. All he ever wanted for Christmas and birthdays was more of the same.

He smiled wryly. 'Dire threats from everybody whenever I said I wanted to become a professional photographer! I would starve to death unless I could make it as a commercial photographer, but that's not what I wanted. I didn't want to work on assignment unless I chose to. I wanted to be a fine-art photographer, take my own pictures and sell them. I didn't want anyone telling me what to do. I said I didn't care if I starved, which is easy to say when you've never been hungry.' He laughed, his eyes crinkling at the corners. 'The problem was that in those days photography wasn't considered an art form. You couldn't make enough money to buy film. So, out of necessity, I had to do commercial work.'

The waiter came to collect their plates and they were silent for a moment, watching again the scene outside. The tall buildings of the city had made room for the western suburbs stretching out until the horizon with the low orange sun suspended above it.

'How did you go about that? Finding work, I mean?' asked Kristin when the waiter had left. She loved listening to Paul's voice, deep and rich with that funny Australian accent. She wondered fleetingly what an American accent sounded like to an Australian.

He shrugged. 'I did what many aspiring photographers do—I made the rounds of local businesses, insurance companies, advertising agencies, real estate agents, church papers, anyone who would possibly use photos for advertising or promotion. A newspaper offered me a job, and I was so desperate that I took it. I lasted three months. I was photographing car crashes and visiting dignitaries wearing plastic smiles and the openings of new restaurants and office buildings and it was deadly. I hated it. I felt ... suffocated. Then I began to blow up and mount my own photographs. Then I asked doctors' offices, banks, schools, libraries, law firms, churches and anyone else I could think of if I could hang them on their walls. That was the best thing I ever did.'

'Exposure, right?' she grinned. 'And then one day a rich patron of the arts discovered you and decided to promote you, and you'd arrived.'

Paul rolled his eyes and laughed. 'I wish, I wish. No, but I did get some more interesting assignments out of it and I actually did sell quite a number of my pictures. But the prices were so low that it still didn't feed or clothe me. I kept doing commercial work, even though I didn't like it. But at least I was working with a camera rather than sitting confined in an office all day dealing with insurance claims or the world market price of coconut oil.'

The sun was setting, an orange ball sinking below the horizon, colouring the buildings pink and orange and gold. The waiter in his black suit came to light the candle and the intimate glow flushed the white and silver of the table and made the glasses gleam.

Five minutes later the sun had disappeared completely, leaving a pale pink and peach glow on the clouds. The Qantas building with its winged kangaroo floated by.

The food arrived and for a while they ate in silence, watching the magic of the fading light on the town below. The Opera House, all lighted up in glorious composition of light and dark and shadows, came into view. A big white luxury liner aglow with light lay berthed at Circular Quay next to the Opera House. The harbour scalloped around the town, meandering in and out to form bays with the houses overlooking them from high bluffs or sitting close to the shore. Lights sparkled everywhere even though it still was not really dark. The water of the harbour was a lead-blue, the sky a shade lighter. The city sparkled a grey-silver.

'How do you like the wine?' asked Paul. He had ordered a bottle of Australian-produced Cabernet

Sauvignon to go with their meal. Australia, he explained, had some very good native wines, and this was one he liked in particular.

'It's very nice,' said Kristin. 'I'm used to the stuff that comes in half-gallon jugs that you drink from plastic cups.' She smiled. 'I'm afraid I don't know much about wine. It's not something we grow up with, as they do in some parts of Europe. In some states you can't drink legally until you're twenty-one—no liquor, wine or beer. You can fight and die in a war, but you can't have a beer.' She shrugged. 'It's an ongoing argument.'

'Must be your Puritan background,' he said, grinning.

'The poor Puritans get blamed for a lot. I don't suppose Australia has that problem. From what I hear, your ancestors weren't exactly Puritans.'

Paul nodded. 'A hard-drinking lot when they got the chance, I expect.' He smiled. 'Well, let's have another glass and drink to all the poor dead ancestors.' The waiter had unobtrusively appeared and stood waiting, bottle poised.

It was completely dark now. The Opera House was no longer in view and other buildings had appeared, tall and impressive with their lighted signs on top—CAGA, NORWICH, BARCLAYS. The red and white lights of the traffic moved back and forth, the cars small and toylike in the deep distance below. Over it all stretched the sparkling splendour of the cloudless night sky.

Kristin sipped her wine, feeling like a character in a movie. All this luxury of good food and wine and this fairytale view of Sydney all around, and all in the company of an interesting man with eyes that were always looking, searching, penetrating to see deep secrets and hidden meanings.

They ordered chocolate mousse for dessert. It was rich and creamy and tasted like a thousand calories.

'You haven't told me yet how you finally made it,' said Kristin as she spooned up her dessert.

His smile was wry. 'I struggled along for years. Then a writer friend wanted to do a travel story about the Western Australian desert and asked me to come along to take photos.'

They were gone three months. When they returned, his friend had written his story and Paul had the most magnificent photographs he had ever taken. They sold the piece to a big American magazine and received more money than either of them had seen before.

'I'd tried for years to get my images in a gallery in Sydney, but without success. Displaying photographs in an art gallery is a relatively new development and many established artists objected strongly to the idea. But after the publication of our photo-story one of the gallery owners rang me up and invited me to come and see him with my portfolio and discuss the matter.' He smiled, a glimmer of triumph in his eyes. 'I had my first real show, complete with champagne opening. A lot of people came to see my work, and from then on it all began to run in earnest.'

Kristin sighed. 'It must have been so exciting. I wish I had some burning talent.' She paused, then laughed. 'I used to write poetry, but I gave it up.'

'You did? Why?'

'Because it was truly awful.'

'Maybe you're just being modest,' he commented.

She shook her head. 'Oh, no. In college I studied English literature and I joined a poetry group, and believe me, I know awful.'

'What are your plans when you graduate in June?' he asked.

'I want to go to graduate school.' She stopped right there and continued spooning up the chocolate mousse.

'To do what?'

Kristin took a deep breath. 'I want to get a Master's in Library Science. I want to be a librarian.' Oh, lord, it sounded so dull and stuffy! It would be so much more interesting to say she was going into biotechnology or aquaculture or environmental studies or a million other things. But the simple fact was that she didn't want to do any of these things. She wanted to be a librarian—a profession, she was well aware, that conjured up images of prim spinsters with grey buns, glasses and orthopaedic shoes. She met Paul's eyes and saw only interest there.

'Will it take you long?'

'A year if I go straight through, but I think it's better to work in a library at the same time and do it in two.' She paused, smiling faintly. 'What I'd like to be is a reference librarian, which is the top of the cream when it comes to librarians, so it's rather a lofty dream, but I can try. They're the ones that deal with the public and get to scurry around to find the answers to all kinds of weird and bizarre questions. I would like that.'

Paul put his dessert spoon down, laughter in the blue eyes. 'I bet you would, going by the kinds of books you read.'

'What's wrong with the books I read?'

He smiled. 'Definitely weird and bizarre. I happened to leaf through the one I saw you read this morning— the one about the kinky sixth-century queen. . . .'

'Oh, that's nothing,' she interrupted. 'There are books a lot weirder than that one.' And she began to tell him about some that she had read and made him laugh. It gave her the most extraordinary feeling to know that she could make Paul laugh with her tales.

They drove home through the brightly lit city and later through the darkened suburbs full of shadowy trees and bushes. Talking was easy now and her inhibitions seemed to have evaporated. She was conscious of her own heightened emotions, of a sense of anticipation.

The house was in darkness except for the outside light. Paul parked the car and locked it. They went around the back and stood in front of the kitchen door.

'Let's not go inside yet,' he said. 'Come, sit down

with me.' He took her hand and led her over to the
wooden bench under the jacaranda tree. He did not let
go of her hand after they sat down and she did not pull
it away. His hand, big and strong, felt good around her
own.

'It's so peaceful here,' she said. 'It's what I like about
Oregon, you know. So many quiet places—the beaches,
the woods, the mountains. You never have to go far.'

'Not very populated, then, like California?'

'Oh, heavens, no. It's nothing like California at all.
We only have about two million people and the life
style is very different, more simple, more rural. The
income levels are lower, that makes a difference.' She
laughed. 'A lot of retired Californians come to Oregon
to live. They're not very welcome, actually. I think
Oregonians are afraid they'll pollute the place.'

Paul laughed. 'Sounds serious.'

'Oh, it is! There's a movement in Oregon to convince
out-of-staters that Oregon is a great place to spend a
vacation, but no good to settle in. They make it sound
awful. There are all kinds of jokes about the rain. Like
you have to have webbed feet to live in Oregon. Or that
Oregonians don't die—they just rust away.'

Half an hour later they got up to go inside. Paul's
hand rested on the door handle, but he did not open the
door.

'I enjoyed myself this evening,' he said, looking into
her eyes.

Kristin felt ridiculously lighthearted. 'So did I. Thank
you for a wonderful dinner. That was the nicest
restaurant I've ever been to.'

There was a strange, shivering silence. Kristin leaned
her back against the wall of the house, her hands feeling
the rough surface of the brick. The air seemed alive
around them. She looked into his eyes and something
quivered between them. His hands reached up, settled
gently on the top of her head, then slowly trailed down
her hair and neck, coming to rest on her shoulders.

'You have beautiful hair,' he whispered. 'Soft, shiny.'

Her heart thumped wildly in her chest. She stared at the fine stripe of his tie, his collar, his chin, his mouth. His hands on her shoulders exerted the smallest of pressures, drawing her gently towards him. Instinctively she moved, as if drawn by a magnet, offering no resistance.

His face was close—so close that she could feel the warmth of his breath on her mouth. His hands moved up under her hair to cradle her head. Her blood throbbed in her ears and she closed her eyes. She knew he was going to kiss her.

CHAPTER THREE

SHE felt his mouth touch hers, warm and gentle. She stood very still, afraid suddenly he might move away. He kissed her slowly, sensuously, his lips brushing softly, exploring the shape and contours of hers. The world went silent around her. There was only the throbbing of her own heart, and maybe his, she wasn't sure. A private world, this, full of sweet sensations and longings. She had never known a simple kiss could be like this. Her mouth, tremulous, yielded to his and her arms slipped up behind his head. Her body trembled against him and she felt his arms tightening around her back. The tip of his tongue touched the corner of her mouth and her heart jumped crazily.

Then suddenly it was no longer just a gentle goodnight kiss. Paul's hands were on her hips, pressing her intimately against him, and his kiss was full of urgency and fire. The blood pounded in her head and she clung to him dizzily. She was shaken by the feeling unleashed in her, and from her throat came a low, wordless sound.

He broke away abruptly, breathing hard, his hands clenched by his side.

Kristin leaned against the house, her knees shaking.

'Oh, my God,' she whispered. 'I don't know what happened.' It sounded so stupid that she could feel her face grow warm with embarrassment. His laughter was low and amused.

'It's called spontaneous combustion. Pfoof!' His hand came out and gently touched her mouth. 'I've been wanting to kiss you all night, but I hadn't expected it to be quite so . . . so explosive.' He drew her to him again.

Her face against his shirt was hidden from his view, which was just as well.

'We'd better go in,' he said softly. He released her slowly, reluctantly. They entered the house and at the bottom of the stairs he wished her goodnight before he disappeared into the study where a bed had been set up for him.

Paul was packing photographic equipment in his car when Kristin came downstairs the next morning. She watched him through the kitchen window, seeing the sun shine on the short hair and the brown arms, seeing the muscles of his back strain as he lifted and moved things around in the trunk of the car, and warm excitement ran through her. He wore old blue jeans and a red T-shirt, showing the long legs and the trim, lean shape of his body. She liked it. It was a good body, well proportioned and muscular. He turned and noticed her at the window and waved, and she waved back, feeling guilty, as if caught in some improper act.

A moment later he entered the kitchen, running both hands over his hair. 'Good morning. Did you sleep well?'

She caught the glint in his eyes.

'Fine,' she said levelly, trying hard not to let the colour come into her face. This was ridiculous! 'Would you like some coffee?'

'Yes, please. Sit, sit . . . I'll get it. You want one?' He poured two mugs and brought them over to the table. 'Where's your mother?'

'I don't know. Grocery shopping, maybe.'

'Scott not up yet?'

'I guess not. I haven't seen him. With that long trip ahead of us today I hope he doesn't sleep all morning.'

'He might. You'd better wake him up.'

'I'll see.'

It turned out not to be necessary. Five minutes later Scott came into the kitchen bouncing with energy. Half an hour later they were saying their goodbyes.

'I'll see you in a few days,' said Paul, and the tone
of his voice seemed to hold a promise. Or was she
imagining it? He kissed her chastely on the cheek
while Scott watched with narrowed eyes. Moments
later they were in Scott's car, on their way to
Arrawarra.

It was a beautiful drive along the coast, although
they only saw the ocean on a few occasions. Small, low
towns, brick houses with red tile roofs, front porches,
small yards all around. They could have been small
towns in America—the same type of architecture, the
same fast-food restaurants—McDonald's, Kentucky
Fried Chicken, Pizza Hut, gas stations, hardware stores
and supermarkets. Green hills sloped softly in the
background against a shimmering blue sky.

Fruit stalls by the road sold peaches and cherries and
mangoes and strawberries and rock melon and
watermelon, their wares advertised on hand-painted
wooden signs.

'Is it anything like this in Oregon?' Scott wanted to
know.

Kristin nodded. 'Oh yes—more inland some places
look very much like this, except that in Oregon most of
the houses are made of wood. The coastline is very
different, though. We have a road along the coast that's
really spectacular. The coast is very rough and rocky
and really majestic, with rocky outcrops sticking out
into the sea and evergreen forests all over the
mountains. It's beautiful. The coastline here is much
softer and gentler, beautiful in a different way.'

Scott gave her a sideways look and grinned. 'You're
very diplomatic.'

'I'm not! I mean it. This is beautiful, just in a
different way.'

'The western coast of Australia is very rough too,' he
told her, 'great big rocky mountains. Maybe it's like
that.'

The scenery kept changing. Farther north she saw

palm trees and the houses were mainly built of wood. Wooden signs offered cooked prawns for sale. Everywhere now were bait and tackle shops and large dealers selling caravans, or campers. Billboards advertised caravan parks. The road was full of vans, and cars towing boats and campers.

Chinese Take-Away, a sign read. *Fish and Chips Take-Away*. Restaurants were everywhere, many offering take-away food.

'Take-away food,' she commented, 'it sounds funny. In the States we say take *out* food.'

'I think *that* sounds funny—take *out*.'

'You don't eat it *in* the restaurant, you take it *out*.'

'You take it *away*,' he argued.

'Australians are weird people,' she said with conviction.

'If you don't stop insulting us,' said Scott with mock threat in his voice, 'I'll stop the car and deposit you by the side of the road, and I hope no one will give you a lift!'

Kristin grinned triumphantly. 'I don't need a lift. All I want is a ride.'

'I give up,' he said in feigned despair. 'Let's stop for a cup of coffee.'

They found a restaurant in a small town called Swansea and had a leisurely break. Continuing the journey, they crossed the bridge across the glittering blue bay where colourful sailboats skimmed the sunshot water, playing in the breeze.

So many different kinds of scenery—flat land with herds of black-and-white cows, stretches of road lined with pine and gum trees. Kristin peered into the trees, hoping to see a sleeping koala, but saw none. A sign by the road said to watch out for kangaroos. All during the day they had crossed countless little creeks and rivers with exotic, aboriginal names—Wang Wouk River, Kooraingha Creek, Cubba Cubba Creek, Ghinny Ghinny Creek. They went through hills and valleys, past stretches of flatland and through national forests.

Halfway through the afternoon they stopped for a late lunch of fish and chips. They passed through the town of Coffs Harbour, then through hilly country, lush and green. The hills had a strange woolly look in the distance.

'What's that growing on the hills?' she asked.

'Bananas.' He grinned. 'They call this area the Banana Republic.'

'Funny—I never thought of Australia as a banana-growing country.'

'All foreigners ever think of is kangaroos and sheep,' he laughed.

'And I've been here a week and I haven't seen a kangaroo yet.'

'We have some around the caravan park,' Scott told her. 'There's an uncultivated patch of land behind the house and they come there sometimes.'

At six o'clock they arrived at the camp. Scott's partner, Stan, was a funny little man with penetrating black eyes, a bushy beard and a floppy hat pulled low over his face. He was bare-chested, wearing shorts and thongs only, and his English was so heavily accented, Kristin could only make out about one word in five.

Kristin was certainly welcome to stay at the house, he said, but unfortunately it was little more than a run-down shack. They hadn't had the time to do anything about it, so they lived in it as it was. She would be more comfortable in a tent.

A tent—oh, yes, she'd much rather sleep in a tent!

Scott had reserved a small lot for her, near the beach. From somewhere in the dilapidated house they unearthed a little tent and Scott put it up for her. Other camping gear was in the back of the car, and an hour later she was all installed. There was wood near the fireplace and she made herself a roaring fire while Scott took off to see about his duties. Stan had sent his girl-friend, a short, big-breasted brunette by the name of Tootsie, in a truck to pick up some fish and chips in Arrawarra. When she came back they all sat around the fire and ate the fish straight out of the newspaper it was wrapped in, washing it down with beer.

Later that night Kristin lay curled up in her sleeping bag and listened to the sounds of the waves washing ashore and the wind whispering through the trees. All around her tent mysterious life was going on in the dark—nocturnal creatures scurried through the greenery, issuing eerie chirps and whoops and cries. She liked the sounds of outdoor life. She wished Paul was with her. Her stomach contracted at the thought of him, and impatiently she turned in her sleeping bag. 'Don't be an idiot,' she muttered out loud. 'Go to sleep!'

She swam and lay on the beach and got a tan. Scott was very busy and she helped him with his work when she could. She read a book a day. At night she lay in her tent and listened to the sea and thought of Paul.

New Year's Eve came. A large pit had been dug and at six in the morning a pig and a lamb were put on the fire to roast. Kristin's mother, Uncle John and Paul arrived late in the afternoon. They all came climbing out of Paul's car, looking tired, but smiling, and her heart leaped at the sight of Paul. His eyes searched for hers, and seeing her, he smiled a private little smile that made the breath catch in her throat.

A caravan had been made ready for her mother and Uncle John. Paul declined the offer of sharing the house. He had brought his own tent, the one he had used for months on his tour through the desert a few years ago, and he pitched it near Kristin's tent. It looked worn and faded and not at all secure. But this was no serious camping here, he said, just lolling by the sea. He grinned at her frowning face.

The others had left and they were alone. The roasting pit was not far away and the smell of cooking meat wafted through the air.

'I'm hungry already,' said Kristin. 'I've been smelling this all day.' She was sitting in a beach chair, knees pulled under her chin.

'You're brown,' he said, eyes sliding down her face and legs. 'Are you enjoying it here?'

She nodded, feeling selfconscious under his regard, then she got up out of the chair. 'I'll get us something to drink.'

Paul stretched out on the grass, arms under his head, and looked at her through half-closed lids. 'Good idea. Let's crack a tube.'

He was trying to trick her with that Aussie idiom, but he wasn't going to. She felt jubilant, but was determined not to show it. The first time she had heard that one from Scott, she had been at a loss as to what he was saying. *Let's have a can of beer*, was what it meant.

Aware of Paul's expectant regard, she tried to look casual as she fished two cans of beer out of the ice chest. 'Here you go.'

He laughed as he took the proffered can. 'Well,' he said, 'I believe we'll make a fair dinkum Aussie out of you yet!'

She laughed at him and shook her head. 'Not a chance!'

One dark brow rose in question. 'No? What's wrong with Australia?'

'It isn't America.'

A smile tugged at the corner of his mouth. 'Well, I can't argue with logic like that.'

Scott came by a while later, looking hot and dishevelled. Obviously he had been tending the roasting meat. 'It'll be ready in about an hour,' he said, quickly draining the can of beer Kristin handed him. A moment later he was gone again.

Paul built a fire and Kristin set the camp table. Her mother came over with a big bowl of potato salad that she had brought all the way from Sydney in an ice chest. There was wine and beer and crusty bread rolls, and when the high sign came they were ready to stand in line for their meat. Scott was passing out chunks of lamb and had put on a high white chef's hat for the occasion. That in combination with his bare chest made quite a picture. All the campers were in great spirits, some already slightly merry, which was less than encouraging, if not unexpected.

The four of them sat around the fire with their paper plates on their laps and ate. Scott could not join them as he was still doing his duty at the roasting pit. The lamb was delicious, but Kristin found it hard to pay much attention to the food. More than once her eyes met Paul's and she was aware of a tension building up. Never had anything like this happened to her before. All around them was laughter from the other campers and the bawdy songs of a group of middle-aged men who seemed to be having the time of their lives. But all she really heard and saw was Paul—his voice, his eyes, the movements of his body as he ate and talked.

It was a wonderful evening, with fireworks on the beach after the meal was finished. They sat in the dark watching the bright colours explode high up against the dark of the sky. The atmosphere was charged with excitement, and children and grown-ups alike shrieked with delight at the magical display of light and colour.

At midnight everyone wished everyone else a Happy New Year, and hugging and kissing abounded. Paul grasped Kristin's hand and pulled her away from the crowd and took her further down the beach.

'I like to do my kissing in private,' he said, pulling her down in the sand and kissing her hard. 'Happy New Year.'

'Happy New Year,' she said.

'Kiss me,' he whispered.

'I already did.'

'I kissed you first.'

'It's too dark—I can't find you.'

'Use your hands, find me. See, I have no trouble finding you.' His hands slid down her shoulders, gently stroking her breasts, and she moved away from him immediately.

'Don't,' she muttered. The blood pounded in her head.

The dark bulk of him reached out for her again, drawing her close to him. 'What do you mean, don't?' He kissed her again, his hands firmly holding her head so she couldn't move. Then, slowly, he pushed her back until she lay stretched out in the sand and he was leaning over her, his mouth still covering hers.

He withdrew slightly, leaning back on one elbow, looking down on her. It was too dark to read his face. One finger trailed gently over her skin, behind her ear, down her shoulder, along her collarbone. The hand lifted away from her and came down on her stomach, moving up under her T-shirt. The touch of his hand on her bare skin tingled through her.

Her reaction frightened her. It was as if all resistance simply faded, as if all she wanted was just to kiss him and touch him and feel him. As if nothing else mattered. Her heart was racing and she felt weak and warm all over.

Paul's hand moved up and covered her breast, and she moved away from him with a muffled cry, pushing at his hand.

He released her and sat up. 'You don't want me to touch you?'

Kristin sat up, pulling her shirt down. She took a deep breath. 'No. . . .'

His laughter was faintly amused. 'It doesn't sound very convincing.'

She clamped her teeth together, feeling anger rise inside her. 'Don't make fun of me!'

'What's the matter?' His voice was gentle. 'Is there someone else? A man at home?'

'No.'

'Is something wrong?'

She shook her head. There was nothing really wrong, she just didn't want to lose her head too easily and too quickly. Paul had the most devastating effect on her nervous system and in the face of all those volcanic emotions she felt hopelessly inexperienced. She hunched her shoulders. 'I'd rather just take it a little easy.'

There was a silence. She was glad it was dark. There was the sound of the waves rushing to the shore and in the distance, faintly, the voices of people. She dug her hands under the sand. It was cold on her skin. Paul was next to her, a dark shape without distinct features.

'Why?' he asked at last, his voice even.

'I don't like rushing into things.' She bit her lip hard. She felt inept and awkward and miserable and angry with herself. She sounded like a confused fifteen-year-old, and it infuriated her. Oh, God, he probably thought she was a real case! Well, she didn't care. She jumped up and wiped the sand off her jeans. 'I want to go back.'

He took her hand. 'You don't like the idea of ending up in my tent, or me in yours, the first time we're alone. Right?'

'Right.'

'It would be very easy.'

Kristin swallowed. Yes,' she admitted.

'Well, nobody says we have to. There's still this old-fashioned idea of getting to know each other a little first.'

She peered up into his face. It really was quite dark. 'Are you serious?'

Paul sighed. 'I wish I weren't.' Then he laughed and tugged at her hand. 'Come on, let's go back.'

They walked back to camp along the water's edge. Now and then tiny waves washed over their feet. Kristin wondered about this mountain of a man beside her, if he really wanted to sleep with her or if it was all

just a game to him. Not long from now she would be
safely back on the other side of these Pacific waters,
and to him it probably wouldn't matter one way or the
other.

Back at the tent site, she gathered towel, toilet bag
and a change of clothing and made for the showers.
There were only two other women there, one in the
shower, the other brushing her teeth with vigour.
Kristin took her time, hoping Paul would have gone to
bed by the time she returned.

He hadn't. He was sitting in a chair, bare-chested, with
some sort of ankle-length cloth wrapped around his
waist. Leaning back with his hands behind his head, he
was staring up into the sky.

'Anything exciting up there?' she asked for something
to say. He lowered his gaze to her.

'Only a sliver of a moon and a million stars, give or
take a few.'

Zipping open the tent, Kristin dumped her things
inside and turned her head in Paul's direction. 'I'm
checking in. Goodnight, Paul.'

He reached out a hand. 'Come here.'

Her legs moved and the rest of her body followed, as
if someone was steering her by remote control. He
grasped her around the waist and lifted her on to his
lap, enfolding her in his arms.

'Don't look so serious,' he whispered in her ear.
'Falling in love is supposed to be fun.' Then he kissed
her softly on the lips before releasing her and sliding her
off his knees. 'Goodnight, Kristin.'

She lay in bed, but couldn't sleep. Music was still
going strong somewhere in the camp—songs from the
fifties and sixties. People were still up, shouting and
laughing and drinking. She wondered if Paul was going
to sit there staring up at the sky for a long time. Finally
she heard him zip open his tent. The noise around
slowly abated and by the time it was almost four she
dozed off.

The next few days were the happiest in Kristin's life. She was hopelessly in love and she knew it. Paul did not stop kissing her and he did not stop touching her, but she was aware of his restraint. It was not easy, and at times she wanted nothing more than for him to stay with her in her tent. She wanted to make love more than anything she had ever wanted in her life, yet some invisible force kept pulling her back.

They swam, they lazed on the beach, they went on late-night walks and early-morning birdwatching expeditions. He taught her how to make dampers—flour-and-water dough wrapped around the end of a stick and cooked over an open fire. They ate fish and chips and barbecued lamb chops and local bananas, and drank Australian wine. They raced each other across the sand, kissed in the moonlight, talked till all hours of the morning, sitting around a campfire. But every night she went to her tent and he went to his.

He told her about his travels and how, not long ago, he had met misfortune on the rocky cliffs in Western Australia and slashed his cheek.

'That scar makes you look mysterious,' she told him. 'And sexy.' She traced it with her finger.

He rolled his eyes. 'That's why I'm keeping it.'

'Aren't you going to do something about it?'

'Like plastic surgery, you mean?' He shrugged nonchalantly. 'Perhaps one day I will.'

His indifference pleased her, she wasn't sure why.

Whenever she came across Scott, he gave her wounded looks. However, he did not seem to be suffering from lack of female attention. Kristin had noticed several giggling teenage girls following him around everywhere like lovesick puppies, and on a couple of occasions she found him in the company of a dark-eyed beauty who paraded around all day in the skimpiest of bikinis.

Paul took hundreds of pictures, and the sheer number of them amazed her. He photographed the rocks and the sea and the flowers and the tiny crabs that scurried out of their holes at low tide at night and made fascinating designs in the sand.

He took pictures of Kristin, usually when she wasn't aware of him, and she didn't mind. They were the kind of pictures no one had ever taken of her—of her toes and her sandy stomach and her back wet with water.

He talked to her about composition, lighting, contrast, angles, lenses. He made her see things she had never seen before, and it was as if a new world opened up with the wonder of it.

And all of it was magnified by her tumultuous, glorious feelings for Paul—a blossoming of love so wonderful she knew that nothing would ever be the same again.

She awoke to the sounds of birds and the fresh morning breeze puffing the curtains through the open windows. She had been back in Sydney for several days now, back in the yellow room in the brick house.

Sunshine and warmth. Another lovely day. Only four more to go and she would be back on a plane to Oregon and winter. She sat up, feeling funny. It was the third day in a row that she had felt sick in the morning. Each day the panic grew. She got up slowly and opened the door, then suddenly bolted across the hall into the bathroom and reached the toilet just in time. She retched miserably.

It had been as bad as this before.

Back in bed she lay very still with her eyes closed, trying to remember, trying to count. It was no use. Rick's image flashed through her mind and again she thought of the night he had said goodbye to her, that last fateful night before he had left.

She knew she was pregnant.

CHAPTER FOUR

HER panic was so intense that she couldn't think or breathe. Huddled under the covers with her eyes tightly shut, she fought the terror. At last she struggled up, gasping for air, and straightened up in bed. She stared at the yellow curtains.

Pregnant. *Pregnant!* It isn't fair! she thought. *It isn't fair!* Oh, God, what am I going to do? She thought of her mother, of Paul, of going back to school, of supporting a child. She thought of not having it. She thought of Rick who was no longer alive and of his baby inside her who was very much alive.

For an hour she lay in bed, her stomach queasy, her mind a wilderness of fear. Maybe I'm wrong, she thought. Maybe I'm overreacting, jumping to conclusions. Maybe it's the water, or some weird Australian virus.

But she wasn't wrong and she knew it. The symptoms were unmistakable, and she knew her own body too well to be fooled. With all her strength she tried to calm herself.

Her stomach needed attention. What was the remedy for morning sickness? Tea and crackers. Slowly she put her feet on the cool wooden floor, then with her stomach churning she wrapped her robe around her and slowly went down the stairs. She hoped fervently that the kitchen would be empty so she could help herself unobserved.

She was in luck. Quickly she heated some water and rummaged through the cabinets for a tea-bag and crackers. Having found them, she carried cup and plate up the stairs and crawled back into bed.

She munched the crackers and sipped the hot tea. It

seemed to help, and she began to feel better—at least physically. She tried to sleep some more. Maybe it was all just a cruel nightmare. Maybe when she woke up it would all be gone. She dozed off. Drifting back to consciousness an hour later, she heard her mother vacuuming downstairs. She sat up, noticing the empty teacup and the plate with cracker crumbs. Facts. Reality. It had not been a bad dream.

There was no way but to get up and face the world as if nothing was wrong. She couldn't very well stay in bed all day.

She showered and dressed, putting on white shorts and a flowered Hawaiian shirt, the bold, vibrant design belying her mental state. An aunt and uncle had vacationed in Hawaii some years ago had brought it back for her. It was much too flamboyant and not at all her style, and she hardly ever wore it. Gazing at herself in the wild-coloured thing, she wondered what psychological significance could be drawn from the fact that she had picked it out to wear today. Then she shrugged and went downstairs once more. Passing the living room on her way to the kitchen, she noticed her mother dusting bookshelves. She looked up and smiled at Kristin.

'Good morning. I was wondering if you'd ever get up.'

'I guess I was tired.'

'Have some breakfast. The coffee pot is still on. When I'm done with this I'm going grocery shopping. Want to come along?'

'Sure.' Doing something, anything, was better than sitting around the house going crazy with panic. Kristin poured a cup of coffee, but couldn't face drinking it, so she drained it down the sink and made another cup of tea. She chewed a piece of toast with mango jam and stared out the window. The thought of frying eggs and bacon made her sick. One slice of toast was all the breakfast she could manage.

Three more days and she would have to leave. Oh, God, she thought, may they pass quickly.

Paul came that night to take her to his apartment for a meal he was cooking himself, and to show her around his darkroom/lab. She was grateful her stomach was fine, even though the rest of her felt wretched. She was tense and nervous all through the meal, conscious of his eyes observing everything.

He reached for her hand across the table. 'Why are you so jumpy?' he asked.

'I'm not,' she lied.

For a moment he looked at her in silence. 'Are you afraid now that you're here alone with me I'm going to try to seduce you?'

She shook her head, suppressing an hysterical laugh. Today the thought of seduction hadn't even entered her head.

Paul got up and came around the table to her side and drew her up out of the chair. 'I wouldn't mind at all, you know—seducing you.'

She said nothing, standing woodenly in his embrace. He bent his head to hers and kissed her softly. 'I want to make love to you very much. I don't know how long I can go on being such a good boy scout.'

'I'll be gone in three days,' she reminded him.

'Won't you tell me why you're worried?'

'I'm not.' Her voice sounded strange.

'You're behaving very strangely tonight.'

'I have a headache,' she muttered. 'I'm sorry.' Lies, lies. Oh, how she hated the deception! She'd been doing it at home too. Her mother had commented that she didn't look well, and she had lied then, too, while all the time she had wanted to tell all. *Please help me, I don't know what to do. . . .* But she couldn't bring herself to tell her mother. She didn't deserve to have a pregnant daughter complicate her life now that she had finally found some happiness of her own. She was alone. Somehow she would have to get through this on her own.

Paul didn't mention it again that night. After dinner he showed her his lab where he developed and printed his photographs. He talked to her about chemicals— developers, stop baths, fixers; about enlarging prints, light exposures and many other things, but in her mind all she heard was, *I'm pregnant! I'm pregnant!* She had wanted to know about his work. In Arrawarra she had asked him if he would show her around some time, but now it took an effort to show enthusiasm, and she knew he was aware of it.

He kissed her when he took her home and she clung to him, desperately, fighting tears. *Help me! Please, help me!* she pleaded silently. But Paul was the last person on earth she could ask for help. How did you tell the man you were in love with that you were pregnant with another man's child?

'Kristin. . . .'

'I'm all right,' she said hastily, voice thick. 'Really I am.' Then she swiftly disengaged herself and ran inside and up the stairs to her room.

She hardly slept that night. She rolled from one side to another, the unanswerable question echoing through her mind all during her restless sleep—*why? Why? Why?* It was a fruitless question. It had happened. It was all that could be said. Over and over again her thoughts kept going back to Rick and that last night together.

He had had girl-friends by the dozen. He was charming, intelligent and entertaining company. Between Kristin and him there had never been more than a close friendship that had peacefully coexisted right along with his romantic adventures. For whatever reason, romance had not featured in their relationship. What they had between them was special, more lasting than his flings, which were always shortlived. In December he had got his Master's degree and, almost at the same time, a job offer in North Africa.

Saying goodbye was terrible. Six months earlier Kristin's mother had gone to Australia, and now Rick

was leaving. She felt suddenly overcome with loneliness.
They stood in front of her window watching the first
snow drifting down and she had thought about the
long, cold winter ahead, about not having Rick to talk
to any longer. He had put his arm around her
shoulders.

'I'll miss you, little mouse,' he had said, and to her
horror she had broken into tears. He had held her for a
while and then he had kissed her.

And that night had not ended like all the other nights
they had been together over the years—with Rick
leaving. That night he had stayed with her, the only
night ever. And how it had happened she still did not
know till this day, for she had always thought of him as
a friend, not a lover.

Afterwards he had been full of remorse, which had
struck her as funny, because after all, wasn't she the one
who was supposed to feel regret?

She hadn't been sure what she felt, except maybe
some vague sense of relief that her initiation into
womanhood was over and it hadn't been a terrible
ordeal. She remembered the look of distress in Rick's
face, could still see it in her mind's eye, still hear his
words.

'I'm sorry, Kristin, Oh, God, I'm truly sorry. I didn't
think. . . .'

'It's all right,' she said, suddenly embarrassed by her
nakedness, by what had happened.

'It's not all right, Kristin. I never intended to . . . to
. . . seduce you.'

She laughed then, a little shakily. 'You did *not* seduce
me Rick. It happened—it just happened. And I don't
mind,' she said softly. 'I'm glad it was you. Who's ever
heard of a twenty-two-year-old virgin, anyway?' she
added on a lighter note.

He didn't smile. 'I feel rotten. I only hope you won't
regret it later.'

She grasped his hand, looking into the warm brown

eyes. 'I won't,' she said emphatically. 'Never. You're the best friend I've ever had, Rick.'

And Rick had left for Tunisia the following day and five days later he was dead. And Kristin, without knowing it, was already pregnant.

The last few days of her stay in Australia took on a nightmarish quality. Her morning sickness was not too severe, but she still needed the tea and crackers and she needed to hide it from her mother. The thought of anyone in the family finding out about her plight was unbearable. All she wanted now was to be away from everybody, to be back in her own apartment at home, to calm down and decide on a course of action.

Paul took her out both nights that followed. They went to the theatre and saw a play one night, and an Australian movie the other. Kristin was grateful for the darkness and the need to be quiet. Still, before and afterwards, there was a lot of time when they were alone as they drove to and from the city, and she tried with all the strength she could muster to act normally. When Paul held and kissed her she would forget everything but her love for him, felt only the urgency of his mouth and hands and body and the sweet, painful longing of her own. Then, as they drew apart, she would be swamped with guilt. She felt like a fraud.

'I'm sorry you have to leave,' he said when they were alone for the last time. His hands were buried in her hair, and he looked down into her face with regret in his eyes. 'If it wasn't because of your degree, I'd do anything to make you stay. You know that, don't you?'

Her mouth was dry. 'Yes.' Was he thinking her depressed state of mind was due to the fact that she didn't want to leave? Well, it would be logical. Not long ago she wouldn't have wanted to. Now it was all she could think of—fleeing from him, from everyone else, being alone in her own apartment to panic in private. Oh, God, she was going crazy! She couldn't wait to get out of here.

'There's a chance I'll be in the States in the autumn,' said Paul. 'Spring for you—April, May. I'll come and see you.'

Kristin gave him a terrified smile. 'April, May?' she echoed.

'A museum in Los Angeles wants to exhibit some of my work, and I'm working on details for exhibitions in galleries in San Francisco and Vancouver. I just received a letter from Vancouver today, and I think the timing will work out.'

'That's wonderful!' Her voice squealed unnaturally, and he gave her a funny look. She turned away and made a pretence of blowing her nose. She had no idea how she managed to get through the rest of the evening.

Paul was at the airport to say goodbye. Kristin felt sick with tension and couldn't think of a thing to say to him. He watched her, the entire hour they had to wait before she could board the plane, his eyes searching her face, seeing, wondering. She felt like screaming. She tried desperately to have a normal conversation with her mother, who seemed a little subdued.

'I wish you didn't have to go,' she told Kristin. 'I wish you'd decide to come to Australia after you graduate.'

'I want to go to graduate school, Mom,' Kristin answered gently. 'Maybe after that. I'll have to think about it.'

This time the trip held no excitement. Nothing seemed interesting any more. Her mind was preoccupied with only one thing, and nothing else in the world was of any significance.

As she emerged from the Portland airport, rain and wind assaulted her. Well, what else was new? Winter in western Oregon meant wind and rain and sometimes snow, and that was what greeted her. It suited her mental state perfectly.

The bus trip back to the university seemed endless. Numbly she stared out the window. The landscape looked colourless and cold, the small towns grey and bleak.

The bus terminal was dirty. A soggy piece of newspaper blew against her leg as she waited for a taxi. It was still raining. It looked as if it might rain for the next ten years.

Her apartment looked dreary and was full of dust and dead air. The contrast between this dingy little place and her mother's cheerful house in Gordon was so extreme that she wondered for a moment how she could possibly manage to live here for any length of time. She stood in the door surveying the room. She'd not known it looked like this, this room of her own she had cherished. Her state of mind coloured her life, her hopes, the very objects around her. What once had looked comfortable and cosy now looked dull and cheap and worn.

She dumped her suitcase on the floor and, without taking off her parka, went around opening windows to let in some fresh air. It was freezing cold. She'd get it warm later, but first she needed to buy some food. Picking up her handbag, she plodded down the stairs and out into the street once more. She trudged through the rain to the supermarket, two blocks down the road. Her legs felt like lead. It seemed days since she had last seen a bed.

Everything looked grey—the houses, the street, the bare trees, the dead grass, the slushy remnants of once-white snow. The rain stung her face and it ached with the icy cold. It was a relief to enter the over-lit supermarket. At least here was some warmth and colour. Quickly she moved through the familiar aisles, filling the cart with milk and tea and crackers and eggs and bread and canned chicken soup.

'Terrible day,' the girl behind the cash register commented cheerfully. She had a mouthful of shiny braces, a face full of freckles and an abundance of bright auburn hair. 'I hope it stops before my shift is over,' she added.

Kristin nodded. She wasn't in the mood for small talk right now. She clutched the paper bag against her chest and set off for home, sloshing through the puddles, shivering. Her feet were cold, she was soaked all through and she felt exhausted.

Back in her apartment she closed the windows, drew the curtains and turned up the thermostat. The place looked unlived-in. Her plants, which were only a few, were at Emma's. She and her husband, Harvey, lived on the floor below. Both of them were graduate students.

Kristin's apartment was an efficiency. There was only one room and the couch was a sofa bed which she pulled out at night after she had moved the rickety coffee table out of the way. The kitchen was in a small alcove, separated from the room by a breakfast bar. The bathroom was minuscule. But small as the place was, it was hers alone; she didn't have to share with anyone. The first two years of college she had lived in a dorm, first sharing a room with three other girls, then sharing with one.

Although sharing had its advantages, she preferred to be alone, having her own place, being her own boss. As an only child, she had been alone much of the time and it was difficult for her to live in such close proximity to other people. At heart she was a loner, although at times she longed for the company of good friends. But good friends were not easy to come by, at least not for her, and at times she felt very alone. She knew it was because she did not give herself easily and kept to herself much of the time.

She took off her sodden sneakers, stripped off her wet clothes and took a hot shower. Wrapped in a warm robe, she heated some chicken noodle soup in a small pan and poured it into a big mug, then, curled up on the shabby blue sofa, an afghan covering her pulled-up knees, she slowly sipped and spooned the hot soup.

She was too tired to think about her problems. The soup finished, she pulled out the couch, made up the bed and went to sleep.

Course registration was the next day, and she stood in line for an hour, paid her tuition, went to the bookstore to order her new books and returned home. Later that day she dropped in on Emma downstairs to pick up her plants.

Emma, her long black hair in a ponytail and dressed in faded jeans and an old sweater of Harvey's that practically hung down to her knees, goggled at her. 'My God, look at that tan—and in *January*! It's obscene!'

Kristin laughed. 'It'll be gone in two weeks.'

The door opened and Harvey came stomping in wearing cowboy boots and a purple parka. A blast of cold air followed him in.

'I'd better go,' said Kristin, reaching for a couple of plants, but Emma took her arm and stopped her.

'Sit down, sit down. Tell us all about Australia.'

She was invited to stay for dinner and help get rid of a colossal pot of chilli.

Emma gave the beans a look of comic despair. 'I wasn't thinking when I made this. It's enough to see us through the rest of the winter.'

Harvey patted her affectionately on the head. 'She'll be a doctor of mathematics in another couple of years, but don't ask her to apply her knowledge in the kitchen!'

When classes began, Kristin settled back in her old routine, but life was not the same. Every morning she woke up feeling sick. Fortunately tea and crackers settled her stomach most of the time. A container of crackers was parked permanently next to her bed and she munched one or two before getting up in the morning. At night she would find the sheets full of crumbs, but was too tired to care. She felt sleepy all the time and could have slept morning, noon and night if she had given in to it.

The weeks went by and January changed into February. The weather was clammy and wet and windy. She worked hard, almost frantically, shutting out thoughts of anything else. At home at night she hunched over her books and studied until she couldn't keep her eyes open any longer.

Her part-time job at the library kept her busy too, although her mind was not very much engaged in the tedious little jobs of shelving books and typing cards for the catalogue and searching the cards for overdue books. She spent little time with friends. For some reason she felt uncomfortable around them, as if she were no longer part of the little group. Her closest friend had been Rick—the others were really just fellow students. She ate lunch with them, discussed assignments, shared notes. She did not confide in them and knew little about their private lives.

She wrote a long and involved paper for a political science course that took an inordinate amount of research and she spent hours in the library looking endlessly through heavy volumes, taking pages of notes.

In the back of her mind she was vaguely aware that she was trying to deceive herself into thinking that everything was normal. She tried not to think about being pregnant. She tried not to think about Paul. But waking up every morning feeling nauseated made it hard to ignore the reality of her predicament. Still, she doggedly kept pushing the thought aside. She plodded through the days with grim determination, going through all the required motions of eating and sleeping and studying and working. How strange to think that there ever had been those glorious days with Paul in Sydney and Arrawarra. It seemed unreal, like some vague, fairytale dream from long ago.

But sometimes memories would catch her unaware, and she would sit on the couch, her knees drawn up under her chin and her arms squeezing her legs against her with a pain so deep she could barely contain it.

One day she received a package from Australia, sender: P. Baldwin. With her heart drumming in her ears, she opened it, her fingers fumbling clumsily with string and paper. A note came fluttering out and she picked it up. *'Thought you might like to have these as a memento of your Australian holiday. I miss you. Keep working, Paul.'* The package contained several large photographs of her on the beach, sandy legs and arms, wet back—strange pictures with strange shadows and highlights. Kristin stared at them, at her own flat stomach on one of them, feeling the misery of the memories seep into her every cell. She put the photographs back in their cardboard frames and stashed them away beneath some old clothes in a dresser drawer.

She sent him a short note of thanks, saying she was indeed working hard and expected he was too.

She wrote cheerful letters to her mother, feeling like a fraud. She received cheerful letters in return, telling her about all the details of her mother's life, about the garden and the new little puppy they had acquired and about helping at a local fund drive by making lamingtons. These, as she described them, were little cubes of cake covered in chocolate icing and dunked in coconut. Her mother had been a 'double dipper', meaning she had to use both hands dunking the cakes in the chocolate icing, and a messier job, she wrote, was inconceivable. She wrote about Scott, who had a new girl-friend, and about Paul, who had taken himself off to Canberra to open an exhibition of his work.

Then, unexpectedly, she received a card from Paul himself. *'Have exhibitions scheduled in L.A., San Francisco and Vancouver. Shall be in U.S. in April and May. Looking forward to seeing you. Paul.'*

Kristin's heart thumped so hard and her hand trembled so fiercely that the card slipped from her fingers on to the floor.

No, she thought. Please, God, no! But in the back of her mind she knew the possibility had always existed. He had mentioned it to her before she had left Australia, but she had pushed it from her mind as she had been trying to push everything else from her mind as well.

The baby: she would have to make a decision about the baby. She was now ten weeks pregnant and it was high time to see a doctor.

The university doctor was a man of about forty with a bushy moustache, an expressionless face and a cool, professional manner. He was new on the staff and Kristin had not seen him before. She disliked him on sight.

In a toneless voice she told him she was pregnant. After a few questions and an examination he confirmed this. When she had dressed again he told her to sit down. He was sitting behind his desk, looking through her file.

'You're not married, are you?' he asked coolly.

'No,' she answered woodenly. Why did he ask? He could read, couldn't he?

'You're about ten weeks pregnant, maybe eleven,' he continued. 'A little late in the game. Have you decided what to do?' He wasn't looking at her.

'Yes,' she heard herself say, not knowing until that moment that she had.

'Do you intend to terminate the pregnancy?' He raised his eyes and gave her a level look.

'No.'

His face remained impassive. 'Does the father know of your intentions?'

'No, he doesn't.'

The doctor's cool, impersonal manner did not invite confidences. Right now she could have used someone to confide in. Her mind was in turmoil, as if all the hidden and suppressed thoughts and emotions of the last weeks were emerging all at the same time. She swallowed and forced herself to look at him.

He was tapping a pencil on the desk as if bored with the whole thing. 'You realise,' he lectured, 'that having a baby may seriously. . . .'

'I know, Doctor. I'll have to work something out.'
She wanted to get away from him. She didn't like him.
She wished she hadn't come.

'It would be wise to talk to one of our counsellors,'
he said, looking at her fixedly. 'You may not have
thought of all the consequences.'

Probably not. She stood up, smiling politely. 'Thank
you, Doctor.' Quietly she left the room.

Kristin went to see the counsellor several weeks later.
The woman was in her late twenties, wore skin-tight
jeans and had an over-abundance of frizzy blonde hair
of the bleached variety. The room was small, furnished
with only a few chairs and a desk hidden under a ton of
paper. The grey walls were decorated with brightly
coloured posters full of warnings and advice about
drugs, pregnancy, V.D. and alcoholism. It had never,
ever, occurred to Kristin that one day she might be in a
room like this, needing help.

'I'm Sandy,' the counsellor said cheerfully. 'Please, sit
down. Would you like some coffee? A Coke?'

Kristin shook her head. 'No, thank you.' Her voice
sounded dull and lifeless. Somehow the woman's
cheerfulness seemed offensive.

Sandy poured herself a cup of coffee from a large
coffee machine, then, balancing herself on the corner of
the desk, she smiled at Kristin. 'Tell me why you're
here.'

Why *was* she here? Her problems were nobody's
business, least of all this thin, frizzy-haired woman with
her pale blue eyes. She was a stranger. The urge to flee
was so strong Kristin almost got up, and she clamped
her hands on the armrests of the chair to keep herself
down.

'Don't feel shy,' the woman said softly. 'You're not
alone, you know.'

Some comfort that was!

Not looking at her, Kristin told her in a few short

sentences. She wondered what the woman thought behind that friendly, concerned façade. *Another one stupid enough to get herself pregnant. Don't they ever learn?*

'Why did you wait so long to come here?' Sandy asked gently. She sipped her coffee, looking at Kristin intently.

'There was no point in coming earlier.' Kristin wondered if she had waited so long because the decision whether to have the baby or not was now taken out of her hands—it was too late for an abortion now. Had she subconsciously not even wanted to consider the possibility, even though knowing that in many ways it might be the best solution for everyone concerned?

She thought of Rick with his boyish charm, his laughing eyes, his enthusiasm for life. She remembered that last night and the remorse in his eyes. He was the best friend she had ever had. Now he was dead, while part of him was still alive inside her, and she could not, would not, have that destroyed too.

'You realise it's too late for an abortion now?' the woman asked.

'Yes,' she said stonily. 'I want to talk about practicalities.'

'First, let me ask you, what does the father say about this? Does he know?'

'He doesn't know.'

'Are you going to tell him?'

'No.'

'Don't you think he should carry some of the responsibility too? At least financially?'

'I can't ask him for anything,' said Kristin.

'Is he a married man?'

'No.' She swallowed. 'He's abroad. I won't see him again.' A partial lie. If she told the counsellor he was dead, she might guess Rick's identity. Several students had worked on the same dig with Rick in Tunisia and his death had been a shock to the entire student body.

'What about your parents? Can you ask them for help?'

She shook her head. 'My father is dead and my mother is remarried and lives in Australia. I'm on my own.'

There was silence for a moment.

'Do you want to keep the baby after it's born?'

Kristin gazed blankly at the floor. 'I don't know.'

'If you can't, or don't want to, adoption is a good solution,' Sandy said quietly. She began to elaborate on the technicalities, while Kristin, silent, listened. She stared at her hands, twisting in her lap, forcing herself to hear the things being said. Financial help for hospital and doctor's expenses was sometimes available. The baby would go straight to its adoptive home and it would have welcoming parents ready to give it all the love and care it needed. She herself could continue her life and her studies without the burden of an unexpected child.

'What were your plans before you knew you were pregnant?' asked Sandy.

'I was planning to go to graduate school.'

'The baby is due early September. It won't work out very well, will it?'

'No.'

'Have you thought of how to support the baby in case you decide to keep it?'

'I'd have to find a job,' explained Kristin. 'I could stay in the apartment I'm living in now. I'd have to find a babysitter, of course.'

But what kind of job would she be able to get that would pay enough to feed and clothe the two of them? And when Sandy asked her the same question, she shrugged helplessly.

'A Bachelor's degree in English literature doesn't prepare you for a lot of practical jobs,' she said. 'I'm working in the library part-time, but I'd need a full-time job to squeeze by. I could get a job as a waitress. I grew up in a restaurant and I have a lot of experience. Maybe, if I can get a job in the right kind of place, I could manage.'

Sandy nodded. 'There are organisations that can help.' She put down her coffee cup and slipped off the corner of the desk. Searching through the heaps of paper on the desk, she extracted a stack of leaflets and brochures and handed them to Kristin. 'Read these. There's a lot of information in them about the agencies—Birthright, White Bird Clinic, etc. And of course, if you like, you can come back here any time and talk some more, okay?'

Kristin took the papers and came slowly to her feet. 'Thank you.'

Sandy smiled. 'I know it's not easy,' she said gently. 'Do take care of yourself.'

A watery sun peeped out between the clouds as Kristin emerged from the building. She took a college bus and rode up the hill to the library to work her two-hour shift.

She examined herself in the mirror regularly, and by the end of March her pregnancy was showing itself clearly, at least to herself. Her jeans had become too tight weeks ago and for a while she had worn them with the button undone, and loose, checked flannel shirts covering her front. Eventually there was no solution but to buy maternity jeans with a soft elastic panel in the front, and some longer, wider shirts to go with them. She wondered how long it would take before people would start noticing the state of affairs, if they hadn't already.

She bought the clothes without trying them on. At home she pulled on the jeans and looked in the mirror. Then she tore them off hastily and threw them viciously through the open bathroom door straight across the living room. Then, sliding to the floor, she buried her face in her hands and wept.

Time was passing and her nausea had eased off. She was starting to feel better. Well, that was something. Strange, how she was doing well physically, feeling emotionally so rotten and lonely. She had not gone back to see the counsellor. The information leaflets she had read through quickly, then put them away in a drawer and not looked at them again. She still didn't know what to do. Later, she kept thinking, I'll make a decision later. First she wanted to survive her finals and write her term papers and graduate.

Thoughts of Paul slipped into her mind at odd moments, unwanted, but inevitable. She had never been in love with anyone, she knew that now. The experience had been overwhelming, but dwelling on it now was fruitless. It was over; it could never be. His visit hung like a threat over her life, and every time she came home she wondered if she would find him waiting for her.

She studied, she worked, she ate, she slept—exhausted every day. She made sure she ate well, took vitamins religiously. She had gone back to the infirmary to see the university doctor once more. Her blood pressure was fine, her hemaglobin was fine—everything was fine. Except that she felt wretched. The doctor advised her to see a private obstetrician and gave her several names and addresses, and she had called and made an appointment for the following month.

She seemed to live mechanically, automatically, doing what needed to be done, trying not to think and not to feel.

One evening Emma came to see her and accepted Kristin's offer of a cup of coffee.

'I've been studying all day and my eyes are burning,' she complained. 'All I need now is a case of eye strain and I can take a vacation. Oh, bliss! Eyes closed on some beach in the Caribbean. Palms, sunshine, Planter's Punch. . . .' She sighed rapturously. 'I could use it, believe me. I'm so sick and tired of all this academic, theoretical garbage, I could scream! If you don't watch out you forget there's a real world out there. Take my advice and forget about graduate school.' She smiled, only half serious.

Kristin poured coffee. 'Sugar? Milk?'

'Both, please.' Emma jumped up from the couch and sat down at the breakfast bar. 'Listen, we're having a party on Saturday and we'd like you to come.'

Kristin hesitated. 'I don't think. . . .'

'Why not? You look like you need a little diversion. Harvey and I decided to have it because we're both going crazy staring at the books all the time, and we're getting cabin fever. There seems to be no end to winter this year. It's April, for Pete's sake, and it feels like February!' She stirred her coffee. 'Come on, you'll like it.'

Kristin smiled. 'All right, thanks. Can I bring anything? Dip and crackers?'

'No, thanks, everything is taken care of.' Emma looked at Kristin thoughtfully, sipping her coffee.

'Are you all right?' she asked softly.

Kristin looked away. 'I'm fine.'

'You're pregnant, aren't you?'

Her hand shook, and carefully she put her cup down. 'Yes.' She'd wondered how long it would take for someone to make a comment about it; it had to be obvious to everyone by now.

'Do you know what you're going to do?'

'I haven't decided yet.' Kristin looked up. 'Some more coffee?' She couldn't bring herself to talk about it, which was probably a mistake. Except for the counsellor and the doctor she hadn't spoken to anyone about her pregnancy. It wasn't healthy to keep it all inside, she knew, but she seemed incapable of opening up to anyone. She didn't know anyone well enough for such confidence.

'Yes, please,' said Emma after a moment's hesitation. There was an awkward silence as Kristin poured the coffee. She put the cups down and lowered herself in the chair facing Emma, who looked uncomfortable.

'Have you talked to anybody?' she asked at last. 'A counsellor, or. . . .'

Kristin nodded. 'Yes—I'm all right. I just have to make up my mind.' She forced a smile. 'Tell me, have you found a topic for your dissertation yet?' It was a blatant change of subject and Emma knew it. Ten minutes later, her coffee finished, she stood up to go. At the door she caught Kristin's eye. 'If there's anything I can do to help, let me know, okay?'

'Thank you.' Kristin closed the door and heard Emma's footsteps rushing down the stairs, back to her own apartment and her husband and companionship and safety.

She took the cups and washed them, wondering what it would be like to have someone to share her life with, someone to talk to about her troubles and worries, someone to love.

Saturday night she dressed in a loose kaftan and put on heels. Carefully she descended the steep stairs, feeling slightly off balance. She hadn't worn high heels for months.

The door was opened to her by Harvey, who motioned her inside to a room full of people in a colourful array of clothes. There was the usual contingent wearing jeans and sneakers; a girl in a lime green jogging outfit and wrap-around sunglasses; an African beauty queen with braided hair, gold jewellery and a stunning Technicolor gown. They sat on the floor drinking Gallo wine from plastic tumblers, talking, laughing, munching potato chips. Harvey handed Kristin a glass of wine and she sat down crosslegged on the floor.

The smell of cheap incense permeated the room. She thought of the fresh, perfumy fragrance of the freesias she had splurged on that morning in a whim of defiance. One bunch of supermarket flowers wasn't going to destroy her budget. Arranged in a small glass vase on the coffee table in the midle of the room, they brightened the place with their cheerful yellow and their springy scent.

Someone was telling a joke which seemed long and involved—something about a movie mogul, a monkey and a cheese soufflé. Since she had missed half the story, Kristin did not understand the punch line when it came. Everyone howled with laughter. She felt isolated and alien, as she had felt so many times—left out of the mainstream of life. Things were passing her by and she noticed too late.

She looked around the apartment. It wasn't much different from most other student pads except that Emma had a flair with inexpensive fabric, bright paint, big plants and travel posters. There were two desks with red-painted shelves full of books above them. The couch, undoubtedly as shabby as hers, was hidden under a cheap, washable throw-cover of deep blue. Red cushions for contrast completed the picture. The walls were white and the wooden window frames were painted red. Red-and-blue striped curtains framed the window. It was simple and effective. I should do something about my place, Kristin thought.

Sipping the wine slowly, she observed the other people. A skinny girl with long red hair and a nervous manner was talking agitatedly to a young man with a bushy beard. She gestured wildly, eyes wide, swinging her hair away from her face in unconscious habit. Kristin wished she could hear what she was saying. It seemed to be of paramount importance, to the girl at least. The beard shook his head and answered her, speaking very quietly, not moving. The girl listened to him, tapping her fingers on her glass, biting her lip and tossing her hair back continuously. No wonder she was so skinny, Kristin thought, spending all that energy moving her body this way and that.

'Hi there!'

She looked up at the figure towering over her. He was built like a tanker and had the face of a thug. He seemed vaguely familiar, but she couldn't remember where she'd seen him before. He was swaying a little, waving a can of beer in his hand. Kristin was afraid he might fall over right on top of her and crush her beneath that massive superstructure of his. She moved away uneasily.

'I wanna sit down,' he whined.

'So sit down,' she suggested, irritated at his drunkeness. It was disgusting to see a grown man reduced to a whining little boy.

Clumsily he lowered himself to the floor, spilling beer over his feet and on to the linoleum. 'It just ain't worth it, y'know?' He hiccupped. 'You think you know a person and then you find out you don't know them at all.' He gulped his beer.

Kristin felt like correcting his English. *A person* is singular; *them* is plural. He burped out loud as he squashed the empty can in his massive hand. 'Pardon me.' He grinned at her bleary-eyed.

Emma rescued her. 'Come on, Kristin, I want you to meet somebody.' She extended her hand and pulled her off the floor. 'Sorry,' she said as they moved away. 'He's drunk. His girl left him last week and he hasn't been sober since. I shouldn't have invited him, except that he is a nice guy, really, even if he does look like a Mafioso bodyguard.'

'I think I know him from somewhere, but I can't place him.'

Emma grinned. 'He's a linebacker.'

'Oh, of course. I don't go much for football.' Kristin had only gone to a couple of games last season. She liked basket ball better. It was faster, had more action. The strategic intricacies of football somehow had always eluded her.

Emma introduced her to a scraggly haired young man with wide round eyes and a thin pointed face. He was an ecology student and looked like a frightened fish. Emma talked to him for a moment, then swept off. Neither knowing what to say, they stared at each other in agonised silence. After a few fumbling attempts, Kristin announced that she was going to find another drink and escaped. Why had she come to the party, anyway? She knew no one here. The music was too loud; a few minutes ago some maniac had turned it up and her eardrums were about to burst. She wanted to leave for the peace and quiet of her own room, except that it wouldn't be very quiet with the music bouncing off the walls and rocking the entire building. She sat down at the other side of the room and contemplated a poster of the Taj Mahal.

A girl with mammoth glasses sat down next to her and began a monologue about the inadequacies of men. They were emotional cripples, she maintained; they didn't want to talk about their feelings or even admit they had any. They were so hung up about their manhood, their image, their virility, they couldn't act like normal human beings with flaws and failings.

She rambled on, eyes restlessly moving around the room, apparently not expecting a reply or an argument. Kristin stared at the white marble mausoleum on the wall, longing for her ratty room upstairs and wondering how she could go home without offending Emma.

Ten endless minutes later Emma picked her way towards her, weaving around the sprawling bodies, gingerly stepping over various pieces of human anatomy and avoiding glasses and dishes and ashtrays placed on the floor.

'There's a man at the door asking for you,' she shouted above the din of the music. 'He has an accent—British or something.'

Kristin's gaze flew to the door. Paul! Dark pants, red shirt, brown leather jacket. Blue eyes locking hers. A grin, wide and generous, reaching her across the room, across all those anonymous faces. Her heart gave a sickening lurch and she jumped to her feet so quickly that a wave of dizziness swept over her. Teetering on her high heels, she arched her back to gain her balance and grabbed wildly at the air to take hold of something while everything spun around her. It was Emma who steadied her and kept her from falling.

'My God,' she yelled in Kristin's ear, 'I thought you were going to pass out!'

'It's these stupid heels. My balance isn't what it used to be.'

Paul had advanced into the room and taken her arm. She gave him a terrified smile, her heart jumping wildly, her toes curling in her shoes from sheer panic.

'Hi,' she croaked.

'Hello, Kristin.'

Emma gave them a radiant smile. 'If you're a friend of Kristin's, please stay and join the jollification.'

'I should be getting home,' Kristin said quickly. 'It's getting late.'

Paul remained silent.

'Right.' Emma touched her lightly on the arm. 'I'll see you later.'

Kristin's heart thundered in her chest as she climbed the stairs and her knees almost gave out. Holding on to the railing, she struggled up. She fumbled with the lock until Paul took the key from her trembling fingers and opened the door without a word.

It wasn't until she switched on the light and finally looked at him that she saw how white he was.

CHAPTER FIVE

AVERTING her eyes, Kristin sat down on the bed which she had pulled out before going to the party, and kicked her shoes off. She rubbed her left ankle. Raking a hand through her hair, she came to her feet slowly again and poured herself a glass of water which she drank in a few big gulps.

Paul was staring at her. She met his eyes. There was something awful in their depths, and she shivered. She crawled with anxiety. Her hand cramped nervously around the empty glass resting on the counter. She let go of it and relaxed her fingers. She studied her nails, the drops of water on the counter, the lamp's reflection in the water glass. His silence was frightening, the music rolling up from the downstairs apartment a nightmarish background.

He wasn't going to speak; he was going to stand there for ever, frozen in time, staring at her with that horrible music throbbing all around them.

'Kristin,' he said at last, his voice husky, 'you're pregnant.'

I *know* that, she wanted to say, but was silent.

He moved away from the door, sank down on a chair, put elbows on the desk, face in his hands. 'Oh, my God,' he muttered.

She put water in the kettle. She was shaking all over. 'Would you like some coffee?' She was determined to keep everything calm and un-emotional—offer coffee, peanut butter cookies, small talk. How did he like Oregon? Wasn't the weather terrible?

He didn't bother to answer. 'Does your mother know?'

'No.' She lowered the kettle to the stove, but didn't turn the heat on.

He looked slowly around the room. 'Do you live here alone?'

No, she wanted to say, I share this mansion with two basketball players and a Russian prince. She swallowed. 'Yes.'

'What about the father?'

'There's nothing to say about the father,' she said flatly. 'He's not here. He doesn't know about it and I'm not going to marry him. I'm on my own.'

'What are you going to do?'

Everybody was always asking her what she was going to do. *I don't know!* she wanted to scream. *I don't know! Don't keep asking me that!*

She shrugged, not looking at him. 'I don't know.'

'How advanced are you?'

'Four and a half months. And I don't want a cross-examination!' Tears burned behind her eyes. 'Leave me alone!'

'I came here to see you,' Paul said slowly. 'I've been looking forward to it for months.' He looked at her, dazed. 'I can't believe it. I can't believe this is happening.' He closed his eyes as if in pain. 'Oh, my God, Kristin, what happened?'

'I'm sure I don't have to tell you that,' she said coldly.

'You told me you didn't have a boy-friend.'

'I didn't have.' *He must hate me*, she thought. *He must hate me for what I've done.*

He stared at her. Then he came slowly to his feet and made his way to the door. His eyes, as he glanced at her one more time, were full of anger and regret. Then he opened the door and went out, saying not a word of goodbye.

She was alone.

She sat on the bed, rocking herself, the pain so deep she thought she might die of it.

It happened two days later. Kirstin sat at her desk, studying, when she felt a faint fluttering movement in her abdomen. She held her breath, waiting, but it did not come again. *Quickening*, that's what it was called, she remembered—the first fetal movement felt by a pregnant woman. She gazed blindly at her notes. The baby had moved. It was there, alive inside her and it had moved; she had felt it. She put her hands on her rounded belly and tried to feel the baby's body inside it, but of course she could not. Yet it was there and she had felt it.

I am here. I am yours. Please love me.

For a long time she sat in the chair without moving, her hands resting on her stomach, feeling for the first time tenderness towards the child, a surging of intense emotion. It had finally become real.

'I'll take care of you,' she whispered. 'I'll try and do what's best.'

So far she had read very little about fetal development. She hadn't been able to make herself. It was as if by ignoring the reality it might go away. She did what the doctor had told her to do—eat responsibly and take vitamins. For the rest she didn't want to think about it.

Suddenly she couldn't think of anything else. At the library she read through every book on the subject, fascinated by what was happening, the miracle of it all. The books said the baby was now about nine inches long. Limbs, fingers, toes were fully formed; it had nails and eyebrows and eyelashes. It seemed incredible.

It became difficult to concentrate on her work, which was unfortunate. Finals were coming up and she needed all the time she had to study.

She developed a craving for grapefruit, the large pink ones from Texas—sweet, tangy, juicy. She could stand at the counter in the kitchen and devour two at a time, peeling them and dividing them into sections, the juice dripping down her face and hands. She figured it was a healthy obsession and indulged herself.

The weather had finally turned and spring was in full bloom. Flowers and grass erupted from the moist black earth and trees budded into a brilliant green. The sky shimmered a vivid blue. The air felt fresh and tasted of sea and sun. Walking out in the crisp, clean air made her not at all anxious to go indoors and apply herself to her books. A fragrant breeze wafted past her, stroking her skin and lifting her hair away from her face. She took in deep gulps of air, feeling an unaccustomed excitement beginning to take hold of her. She felt more alive than she had for a long time.

She wished there was someone to talk to, to share what was happening to her. There was no one she knew well enough, no one who was or had been pregnant. Once, in the supermarket, she found herself next to a young pregnant woman looking over the selection of fruit juices, and had the sudden urge to approach the woman, ask her if this was her first baby and how was she feeling and had she been sick in the mornings and was she afraid of the birth and what doctor did she see.

For minutes she stood silently next to her, reading labels, hoping the woman might say something, too inhibited to start a conversation herself. Eventually the woman walked away, giving Kristin only a passing glance.

There were small babies everywhere, and she studied them with fascination, wondering about her own, its features and colouring and size. She observed the mothers too, curious to see how they dealt with their offspring. Some seemed harassed and were irritable and impatient; others seemed happy and talked to their babies, made funny noises and smiled and hugged them close. It awakened in her tender feelings, but doubts and uncertainties too. She hadn't planned on this baby, but would she ever be able to give it away? And if she kept it, would she be a good mother?

She thought of her own mother and wondered what would happen if she told her. Sooner or later, of course, she would have to. Maybe if she didn't keep the baby there was no need to tell her anything. Paul was the only one who knew. But it was a terrible secret to be carrying around with you for the rest of your life. She pushed the thought aside. There was still time to decide.

One night after she came home from the library, she sat down with pencil and paper and examined her financial position. There was enough money in the bank from the sale of the restaurant to last her for a while, but how long was hard to say. Her expenses, if she decided to keep the baby, would be very high. Doctor's bill, hospital cost, all the things she needed for the baby—clothes and a cot and diapers and sheets ... it was a never-ending list. She would have the sofa bed removed and buy a single bed. In the daytime it would have to serve as a couch. With a bright cover and some big cushions propped against the wall it should work all right.

The baby was due in the middle of September. As soon as possible after that she would have to find a job and a babysitter. And then, somehow, make a new life for the two of them.

If she decided to keep the baby.

She was getting tired of Vanessa copying her notes of the seven a.m. English Lit. class. She wasn't eager herself to get up so early, but she did it. Vanessa apparently stayed in bed. A tall blonde with striking green eyes, she was well sought-after by the males of the campus. She lived in a tiny apartment across the street and it was convenient to pop over and copy Kristin's notes.

She was there again the next night, sitting crosslegged on Kristin's faded rug, writing, when suddenly she looked up at Kristin and put down her pen.

'Are you getting married?' she enquired.

Surprised at the unexpected question, Kristin stared at her blankly for a moment, wooden spoon dripping gravy suspended in the air.

'No,' she said shortly, then turned her attention back to the stew.

'I think it's great what you're doing. I mean, having a baby by yourself. Men! Who needs them!' It came out full of contempt. 'I've thought of doing it too, but later, when I've made something of myself, you know. Just skip the whole marriage business. It's so depressing when you look around. It's easier by yourself, don't you think?'

It's easier by yourself. What did Vanessa know about being pregnant by yourself? About not having anyone to talk to, to share the feelings with. About always being alone with your worries and fears. Alone, alone . . . how could it be easier? The loneliness ached in her constantly. Her room seemed filled with its essence. All the hours and days and weeks and months . . . no hand to hold, no one. . . .

Kristin looked at Vanessa, whose face seemed suddenly strangely contorted. She was biting her lip hard and her nails were digging into her palms.

'Men! I *hate* men!' She burst into tears. 'Women are so stupid,' she sobbed. 'How come we're so blind? We fall in love with them and all we see are those gorgeous eyes and those magnificent muscles. And everything they say is brilliant and intelligent and we're so goddamned impressed by their supposed superiority. . . . Oh, yes, we still are. We all want someone to look up to, somebody who's smarter than we are, somebody to reflect glory on *us*. This is the eighties and we're still doing it.'

'You can't blame men for what we're doing to ourselves.' Was she talking about herself too? It would be easy to blame Rick for the trouble she was in now; she had been aware of that from the beginning and consciously fought not to lay blame on him. She had been in full possession of her faculties and he hadn't forced her into anything. Had she refused it would never have happened, she knew that. They had been equal participants. She might never understand how it had happened, but she herself was no less responsible than he.

'They *want* us that way! They want somebody inferior, not quite so smart, so they'll look good by contrast. Haven't you noticed how damned *threatened* they are by women who show they have brains and know how to use them? Ever noticed what happens to men when their wives make more money than they do? They can't take it, you know. Their tender egos shrink from the pressure.'

Kristin stirred the stew absently. 'It seems to me that both parties are equally guilty—the men for expecting it and the women for allowing it.'

'Oh, God,' Vanessa moaned. 'I don't know how I'm going to live with myself. I feel so rotten.'

'What's wrong?'

She laughed bitterly. 'George the Magnificent dumped me.' With a tired hand she wiped the hair away from her eyes. Always soft and shiny, it now looked dirty and stringy. There were blue circles under her eyes. 'Four days ago he says he's going on this motorcycle trip to California for a couple of days and he wants me to go with him. Well, I'm scared stiff of those bikes and I don't want to go on them. I can't make myself. So he laughs at me, calls me all kinds of names, and takes off with this silly freshman....' Vanessa wiped her eyes with her hand. 'So why am I crying? Who needs the bastard? Good riddance!' She produced a fresh supply of tears.

'I'm sorry, Vanessa.' It sounded so inane. She wished there was something she could say that would help, but she couldn't think of anything. She didn't know Vanessa very well; she couldn't throw her arms around her and comfort her. Maybe that's what's wrong with me, Kristin thought in a flash of insight. If I can't give comfort, how can I ever expect to get it? No wonder I'm alone.

'What *is* it with those guys?' Vanessa continued tearfully. 'They don't like to take responsibility for a relationship. They only want what they can get out of it without giving anything back. All they want is action, and no emotional involvement. And then when things go wrong they just bail out. Just look what happened to you!'

Kristin felt a surge of anger replace her pity. Her body grew hot with it. 'Vanessa,' she said with barely contained fury, 'you don't *know* what happened to me. You know *nothing at all* about my circumstances and I would appreciate it if you wouldn't catalogue me or make judgments about me.' Clamping her teeth together she said no more, turned off the stove, all the while looking Vanessa straight in the eyes.

Vanessa lowered her gaze. 'God, I'm sorry. I didn't mean. . . .' She jumped to her feet. 'I just feel so rotten. I'll go for a walk, scream in the wind. I'll come back for the notes another time.' She swung out of the door.

Kristin stared at the stew, the potatoes and carrots and the bright red pieces of tomato. It smelled delicious. She felt sorry for her anger already. Vanessa was feeling bad and she hadn't helped. She ladled some stew into a bowl, curled up on the couch and balanced it on her stomach. Alone. Maybe it was better than all the tears and disillusionment and broken hearts.

Early one evening Kristin was mashing up tuna fish with mayonnaise for a sandwich when the bell rang. When she opened the door Paul was there. Her heart leaped as she looked at the familiar face, saw the deep blue eyes, the scar on his cheek, the short curly hair.

They stared at each other without speaking. From downstairs the spicy smells of Emma's cooking drifted up. The excited tones of classical Spanish guitar danced in the air.

'Come in,' she said at last, and her voice shook. 'I thought you'd gone back to Australia.'

'I was in Vancouver.'

'Oh.' She closed the door behind him and realised her legs were trembling.

He turned to face her, his gaze sliding over her searchingly. 'How are you?'

She pulled her shirt down over her belly and ran her tongue over her dry lips. 'Fine.' She stood frozen to the floor, aware of his regard, aware of her protruding stomach. Her throat ached and she swallowed painfully. 'Please sit down. Would you like some coffee?'

'No, thank you.' He took off his coat and she pointed out the hooks behind the door, then went to heat some water to make some coffee for herself. She needed something to do. Somehow she felt safer behind the breakfast bar where only the top part of her was visible to him.

'I thought you were finished with your exhibitions last time you were here,' she said.

'Only in L.A. and San Francisco. I was in Vancouver these last few weeks.'

'Oh.' She put the bowl of tuna back in the refrigerator and took the coffee off the shelf. A strand of hair fell in front of her eyes and she pushed it behind her ear. She was tired, her hair looked terrible—it always seemed to look terrible these days. She didn't care. She swallowed at the lump of misery in her throat. Why had he come again? Why could he not leave her alone?

'Please come and sit down,' he said quietly, and the tone of his voice made her look up in alarm.

'All right.' She turned off the stove and went over to the couch. Sitting down, she pulled the afghan on her lap and rested her hands on top of it. Paul was sitting on the only chair, looking at her fixedly.

'I want to ask you a question.' There was something terrible in his eyes and the knuckles of his hands were white. She felt a sudden chill of apprehension.

'Yes?' Her voice caught in her throat.

'I want you to tell me,' he said slowly and deliberately, 'whether Scott is the father of your baby.'

Stunned, she stared at him, feeling all the colour drain from her face. *'Scott?'* she whispered incredulously. *'Is that what you've been thinking?'* Coming to her feet, she turned away from him and leaned her forehead against the cool glass of the window. She closed her eyes. Oh, God, she thought in horror, is that what he's been thinking about me? Hopping into bed with Scott the first week I knew him, then falling head over heels in love with him the next?

'Is he?'

She turned in a rage, nails cutting into her palms, breathing fast. *'No!'*

Paul slumped in his chair, all tension suddenly draining out of him. Leaning forward, elbows on his knees, he rested his head in his hands. 'Oh, God, Kristin,' he muttered in a choked voice, 'I thought I was going crazy. I wanted to kill him! It's a good thing we had the entire Pacific between us. The things I did to him in my imagination. . . .'

'What made you think it was Scott? How could you have thought that?'

'Several things. You told me there was no one at home. The timing seemed right. And the fact that he seduces every dolly bird that crosses his path.'

'Well, I'm not a *dolly bird*, and he didn't seduce me,' she said bitterly. 'And to set your heart at rest, he never even tried.' She felt cold. She rubbed her arms and stared at the half-finished psychology paper on her desk.

'I'm sorry,' he said quietly.

Kristin said nothing to that. There was a silence. He wanted her to explain what had happened to her, but she couldn't. The silence stretched. Outside she heard a college bus rumble up the hill past the apartment. The vague sounds of music drifted up through the floor from below.

At last Paul came to his feet, jammed his hands in his pockets and stepped in front of her. 'You told me you were on your own,' he said, looking into her eyes. 'What about the father? Who is he? Why didn't you tell the bastard?' His voice was cold and anger glowed in his eyes.

She straightened herself in indignation. 'I didn't tell him because he was dead before I knew I was pregnant! And he wasn't a bastard!'

Anger faded from his eyes and his expression softened. 'Did you love him?' His voice was quiet now and she wondered what he expected her to say.

She turned her back. 'I don't want to talk about it,' she muttered miserably. *No, I didn't love him, I just went to bed with him.* It would sound wonderful, wouldn't it? She walked around the breakfast bar and turned on the stove again. She needed something hot—coffee, tea, something to chase away the chill inside her.

'I'd offer you a drink,' she said, speaking to him across the bar, 'but I don't have any.'

Paul didn't answer her. Instead, he came up to her and put his hands on her shoulders and looked into her eyes. 'What about the baby? What are your plans?' he asked.

She shrugged, moving away from his touch. 'It's too late now for an abortion.' Abortion: it was an ugly word. *It's all there now, you know,* she wanted to add. *Arms and legs and fingers and eyelashes and nails.*

'I didn't mean that. But why didn't you?' He was leaning against the counter, scrutinising her, and after a quick glance she looked away.

'Have an abortion, you mean?'

'Yes.'

'I couldn't, I just couldn't do it.'

'It would have made everything a lot easier for you.'

The kettle shrieked. She turned off the heat and spooned ground coffee into the filter cone. 'Easy isn't always easy, if you catch my drift.'

His mouth quirked. 'I think I know what you mean.'

Kristin poured water through the filter. 'Obviously you think I should have gotten rid of it,' she said coldly, the words sounding hard and unfamiliar in her own ears.

'I didn't say that, Kristin. I'm only trying to figure out how your mind works, and you're not making it easy.' He paused fractionally. 'An abortion seems to be what many women in your situation would see as the solution.'

'Well, *I* didn't.'

'You don't need to be so defensive,' he said quietly.

'I'm not!' Tears filled her eyes. 'And I don't want to discuss it!' She plonked the kettle back on the stove and stared at the soggy coffee grounds as the water slowly seeped through them into the pot below. Paul left her to it and sat back down in the chair, stretching his legs out beside the coffee table.

How can it be, she thought miserably, that I'm always aching for someone to talk to, and here's Paul, willing to listen, and I just can't make myself open up to him?

She took out cups, milk and sugar. 'Would you like a cup now? There's plenty.'

'Please.'

'Milk, no sugar, right?'

'Right.'

She remembered. She remembered everything. She poured milk in both the cups and added sugar to hers, then carried the mugs to the coffee table. They were cheap dime-store mugs decorated with Irish jokes. She sat down on the couch and tucked her shirt down. It was always creeping up.

'Good coffee,' he commented.

'Thank you. Mountain grown, the manufacturer claims.'

'So is all coffee, good or bad.'

'Really? I didn't know that.'

He pointed at the couch. 'Is that where you sleep?'

She nodded. 'It pulls out into a bed.'

'I believe that's what I saw last time. Not much room in here when it's out.'

'No, but it's fine for me.' She stirred the coffee. 'Where are you staying?'

'A motel—the Blue Star Inn.'

Kristin grimaced. 'A pretty seedy place. Couldn't you find something a little more respectable?'

He shrugged. 'It was the first place I saw. I don't care.'

'When are you going back to Australia?'

They were two strangers making polite conversation. It was safer that way.

'I don't know. The day after tomorrow I fly to Denver, Colorado.'

'Another exhibition?'

He shook his head. 'Not now, but perhaps later this winter—summer, I mean. August. I have an appointment with a gallery director to discuss the possibility.'

'How did you do in California? And in Vancouver?' she asked.

'So far, so good. Sold two images to museums for their collections, and a number to private collectors.' He stood up, restless, stuffing his hands in his pockets again. Then he took out one hand and looked at his watch. 'How about some dinner? Any place around here that serves the famous Oregonian seafood?'

Kristin curved both hands around her mug. 'I have to work. I have to finish my psychology paper by Monday and I'm only half done. I'll have a sandwich.'

Paul frowned. 'You need to eat something better than a sandwich,' he said, and she knew by the tone of his voice what he meant. She had to take care of herself because of the baby. Strangely, she did not resent it.

'I eat well,' she assured him. 'I even take special vitamins.'

'Have you seen a doctor?'

'Of course—once a month. I'm doing everything I'm supposed to do.'

'What does the doctor say?'

'Say?' She shrugged. 'That I'm doing fine. He calls it a normal, uncomplicated pregnancy.' The irony in her voice was hard to miss, but Paul's face registered no reaction.

'Has he or anyone else talked to you about having a baby? What to do after it's born?'

'We've got a roomful of shrinks and counsellors at the university. They tell me adoption is a possibility.'

He studied her for a moment. 'Do you want to?'

She closed her eyes. 'I don't know. I haven't decided anything.' Her voice shook. 'I suppose it's a reasonable solution. Somebody out there is dying to have a child.' Room all ready and decorated. Toys, crib, dressing table, Winnie-the-Pooh pictures on the wall. She'd visualised it in her mind many times. A young couple, waiting, waiting, jumping every time the phone rang. Maybe it would be the agency saying there was a baby for them. A baby to fill the empty space in their lives, in their house.

'Reasonable may not always be desirable.' He paused. 'Kristin, have you thought about going home?'

'Home? To Australia, you mean?'

'Yes.'

'Australia is not my home,' she said.

'It's where your mother is.'

'I can't go there,' she said stonily.

'Why not? Because she's married to my father?'

She shrugged. 'It's one reason. I don't want to upset her life. She's happy now.'

'But you need her.'

'I can manage on my own.' She pressed her lips together in defiance. 'I'm not going there. I'm staying here. I'll be fine.' Her eyes looked straight into his, not wavering. 'And I'm asking you not to tell her about me. I'll tell her myself when I'm ready.'

Something flickered in the blue eyes. 'I don't know if I can promise that.'

Anger flared up inside her. She came to her feet and looked at him across the table. 'You have no right, Paul, no right at all to tell her anything! It's *my* life and *my* private problem, and I'll deal with it the way *I* see fit!'

He stood up too. 'I suppose you're right,' he said calmly. 'I'm sorry, I didn't mean to make you angry, but I'm worried about you, don't you know that?'

Her anger faded as fast as it had come. 'You don't need to be. I'll be all right.'

Paul shook his head slowly, glancing around the shabby room. 'I wish I could believe that.'

'Paul,' she said in a tight voice, 'thousands of women have babies by themselves these days. We can manage without ranch houses and husbands.'

'But not without money or jobs.'

'I'll manage!'

He didn't reply. Crossing the room, he took his raincoat off the hook and turned to her. 'Come on,' he said, 'let's find something to eat.'

Kristin shook her head. 'No, thank you. I have to work.' Bending over, she picked up the empty coffee cups and carried them to the sink. The door opened and closed. When she looked over her shoulder, the room was empty.

She had a tuna fish sandwich, a grapefruit, a glass of milk and a big pink vitamin capsule. Pink—how appropriate, she thought sarcastically. Sweet, sugary, sentimental. Then she took a long, hot shower, washed her hair and, wrapped in a warm robe, sat down at her desk.

She couldn't concentrate. The words blurred before her eyes. Her brain did not produce anything except thoughts and images of Paul. Trying to work tonight was an exercise in futility. It all seemed so irrelevant to the realities of her life.

Everything was such a struggle lately. She worried about the growing baby, kicking inside her. About the future. About the papers she had to write and the exams to take. She felt an ever-growing tension and a draining weariness.

And now Paul. She wished he had not come to see her. Australia, Sydney, Arrawarra Beach—remote and unreal as a dream, and Paul was part of that. Only he wasn't, not anymore. He had emerged into reality and demanded recognition. As soon as she had seen him she knew that her feelings for him were still as deep and real as ever.

Too late now, too late.

Inside her the baby moved, and she put her hands on her stomach for a moment, wondering about that small living being inside that was changing her life and her love. With a wild fling of her arm she swiped the books and papers off her desk and put her head down on her arms. 'My own fault,' she muttered out loud. 'My own stupid fault.'

She felt so achingly, painfully lonely. Her friends were no longer her friends, for they no longer shared her life, her world. She felt so disorientated, so out of place. Her friends thought she was either stupid or heroic, but no one seemed to really see her the way she was. They hadn't had the same experience. They didn't know what to make of her. They either expected her to blame the baby's father for leaving her to cope on her own, or to state bravely that she was pregnant by choice and didn't want marriage. Since she did neither, they were confused.

Stiff and sore, she awoke a couple of hours later. She rubbed her face and ran her fingers through her hair, gazing blankly down on the empty desk in front of her, then stumbling to her feet, she moved over to the window and looked outside. Everything gleamed with rain. The glow of street lamps was reflected in the wet sidewalks and the sky was dark and starless. The clamminess seemed to penetrate the very walls and windows, and she shivered. Quickly she drew the curtains, then bent to pick up the books and papers she had thrown on the floor earlier.

She pulled out the bed and got ready for the night. A numbness had set in and she fell into a dreamless sleep.

Paul came back the next night. When Kristin opened the door to him, he didn't wait for her to ask him in, but entered silently, took off his raincoat and faced her. He didn't sit down.

'Kristin,' he said in a calm, level tone, 'I don't want you to treat me like a stranger.'

'I don't know what you mean.' She looked at the top button of his shirt, feeling herself harden inside in defence, as she had done the night before.

'Yes, you do, Kristin,' he said patiently. 'I came here to see you, and you know why. Yet you treated me as if you wanted nothing to do with me. You don't want to talk to me, you don't want to answer my questions. I want to help you, Kristin. I'm worried about you.'

She tucked a strand of hair behind her ear and gave him a fleeting glance, then looked away. 'Why?'

'I care about you. We had something special, and I don't want it destroyed.'

A bitter laugh escaped her. 'I don't see how we can prevent it. Look at me! Things have changed a little.'

He took a step forward and she backed away. Something flashed in his eyes. 'Don't,' he said quietly. 'Don't be that way.'

'Like what?'

'Bitter, hostile. I'm not the enemy, you know.'

Tears filled her eyes. Why did she have to love this man? Why was everything such a hopeless mess? Memories of sunfilled days flashed through her mind— the lightness and the laughter and the joy of being together, the way he had looked at her, the excitement of his touch.

With a groan he pulled her to him. 'Oh, God, Kristin, I don't care, I don't care about anything.' And then he kissed her. It was the kiss of a desperately hungry man, and fire raced through her blood. There was nothing she could do. Some invisible force held her right there in his embrace, made her kiss him back, cling to him. His body was hard, his muscles taut with restraint. He withdrew suddenly, taking a ragged breath. Tears were running down her face and she was trembling uncontrollably. For a long moment he only looked at her, then slowly his hands moved from her back down her hips around to the front and rested on her abdomen.

She froze. She could feel herself grow rigid. Then she wrenched herself free and took a shaking step back. 'Don't,' she said huskily.

'Why not?' he asked softly.

'*Because!* I . . . I don't want you to touch me!'

He took a step towards her. 'Yes, you do,' he stated firmly. 'You want me to touch you and kiss you and hold you.'

She closed her eyes. 'Please don't.'

'Kristin, you're pregnant. *You* know that. *I* know that. It's a reality we have to deal with.'

She opened her eyes. '*I'm trying to! Don't you know I'm trying to?*' She swallowed painfully. 'Please don't make it more difficult for me than it already is.'

'I want to help you.'

She shook her head. 'Not like that. Please, Paul, not like that.'

'What do you want me to do?'

'I want you to go home. I want you to please leave me alone.'

He was standing right in front of her and there was no place to go. His hands came up and touched her hair, moving his fingers through it. 'I can't. Don't you see? I can't leave you.' His face came closer and he softly touched her mouth with his lips. 'I'm going to stay on for a while.'

CHAPTER SIX

KRISTIN braced herself mentally. 'I don't want you to,' she said, and the words hung in the air for a long, silent instant, belying what she felt in the far reaches of her mind. 'I need to go on with my life and nothing is going to be the way it was—you know that. It's over, Paul.' She thought of all the lazy hours at the beach at Arrawarra, the long walks, the conversations at night around the fire, the shared laughter, the mutual sense of belonging.

Everything had changed.

It was a truth so painful that she tried to harden herself against it, block it out. She didn't want Paul in her life now. It would only prolong the misery.

And all that because she was having a baby. For an instant of bitter regret she willed it away. She didn't want the baby. *She didn't want it!* It was taking over her body, taking over her life. It made her sick in the mornings; it ballooned out inside her and obliterated her shape; it tapdanced on her bladder. No longer was she herself. In everything she did she had to consider the child—eating, sleeping, moving, planning the future. . . . She couldn't run up the stairs or lie on her stomach. Chocolate-covered doughnuts were taboo. She had to drink milk, which she hated. She might not be able to finish graduate school. She had to say no to the man she loved. . . . She had not chosen this pregnancy, and it was intolerable to be taken over so completely. She rebelled against it futilely.

She took a deep breath. It was not the baby's fault— it had nothing to do with it; it was an innocent victim. She should never, never forget that. She only had herself to blame.

'I'm going to Denver tomorrow and I'll be back in a few days,' said Paul as if he hadn't heard her. 'And now, put on a jacket and let's have dinner. I didn't like eating by myself yesterday.'

He stood there, tall and big, hands thrust into his pockets, ignoring her. Anger surged through her. 'You're not listening to me!'

He regarded her, his eyes a deep, intent blue. 'I am,' he said calmly, 'but I'm not going to leave you here like this, and I'm not going to argue about it.'

'What is it you want from me, Paul?' Her body was tensed, her nerves strung taut.

Slowly he shook his head. 'I don't know, but leaving you isn't it.'

'Why? You're not responsible for me or . . . or . . . for the baby.'

'Maybe it isn't a sense of responsibility that makes me want to stay. Why can't you just let it be?'

'Because. . . .' Her throat felt dry and she looked at him, then closed her eyes as if it was easier to speak without seeing his face. 'Because in Arrawarra I was in love with you.' She was embarrassed to hear her voice tremble.

'And in Arrawarra,' he said slowly, 'I was in love with you.'

Kristin opened her eyes and looked at him. There was a tenderness in his face that made her heart swell with emotion. But he was remembering someone else, not the woman she was now, pregnant with another man's child. He was clinging to memories that had no relation to reality.

She looked at him steadily. 'Past tense.'

'I don't want it to be.'

'It has to be. It can never be like it was again.'

'If we can't change with the circumstances it wasn't worth anything. I want the chance to find out if what we had was real.'

It was real, she wanted to say. *For me it was very real.*

But how can you want me now, while I'm carrying another man's child?

'What about the baby?' she asked.

'I don't know. I wish you'd tell me how you feel about it. I wish you'd talk to me.'

She swallowed. 'I don't know how. I . . . I don't want to.' Tears burned her eyes. If only she could have loved Rick in a real, passionate way. If only she could say, *I loved him.* But there had been no grand passion, no magnificent obsession to excuse her for her folly.

Paul touched her cheek. 'Maybe another time,' he suggested gently. He took her hand. 'Come along, let's go and have a meal.'

'I have work to do,' she said miserably. 'I'm in the middle of finals and I. . . .'

'Is your situation so desperate that you can't take time out to eat?' he interrupted. 'We'll make it quick, find a place nearby. Then I'll bring you home and I'll leave. You'll have another couple of hours to study.' He took her jacket off the hook behind the door and draped it around her shoulders. 'Come along now.' He led her out of the door, locked it, pocketed the key and headed down the stairs.

A mild breeze stirred the air. It felt clean and fresh against her flushed face. She looked down at her jeans and sneakers. 'I'm not dressed for anything but the ordinary,' she commented, tugging at her jacket. It would still zip, but only barely. Never mind, soon enough it would be warm enough for just an unbuttoned sweater.

Paul held open the door of a dark blue car.

'Is this yours?' she asked.

'I hired it.'

Rented it, her mind protested, but she didn't voice it. Even the jokes and banter belonged to another time. Kristin slipped into the passenger's seat. He closed the door and came around, moving next to her behind the wheel.

'Where to?' he asked.

'There's Ozzie's, not far from here. It's a seafood restaurant, casual but very good. Where did you go yesterday?'

He turned the key in the ignition. 'A fast food place. I had a hamburger and chips—french fries. Then I went to a film. Terrible, but it passed the time.'

She should have gone with him. She had spent the evening sleeping with her head on the desk. Her gaze settled on the strong brown hands on the wheel and memories of their gentle touch drifted into her consciousness. A pain rose inside her and lodged in her throat like a stone.

They ate abalone steak, baked potatoes with sour cream and a tossed salad. The conversation was strained, the atmosphere uneasy. They were trying too hard to stay away from touchy subjects as they talked like strangers.

Kristin was glad when it was time to go. Paul walked up the stairs with her, unlocked the door and handed her the key.

'Thank you for dinner,' she said awkwardly.

'I'll be back in a few days. I'll cook us a meal here and you can just sit and study and not have the bother.' He leaned forward and kissed her full on the mouth, and she stood there, without moving, until he straightened away from her. There was nothing she wanted more than for him to take her in his arms. She needed his closeness and his loving, and inside her everything cried out for him. But there was something stronger than that, a force holding her back, changing her into a stone statue. It was too late, too late, no matter what he said or thought.

'Goodnight, Paul.' Her voice was a croak and his hand reached out and touched her hair.

'Take care of yourself. I'll ring you up tomorrow.' He turned and leaped down the stairs, taking several steps at a time, his hands sliding down the rails for support. For such a big man he moved with amazing agility.

Kristin watched him disappear into the dark stairwell, then heard the front door open and close. Slowly she turned and went to the window, seeing the lights of the car come on, hearing the engine roar into life. Then he was gone. It was not yet nine. If she applied herself, one hour of study would do for tonight. But she felt drowsy with the big meal inside her, and not even a strong cup of coffee helped. In the end she gave up in frustration and went to bed, setting her alarm clock for five. Her sleep was restless and full of confusing dreams.

The obstetrician Kristin was now seeing for her monthly check-ups was a kindly man, a little short, with warm brown eyes and a gentle manner. He told her she was doing just fine. The baby's heartbeat was now clearly audible. He had a gadget that magnified the sound, and when she heard the quick pulsing beat her throat suddenly thickened. More often now she felt the baby move inside her, and hearing the sound of its little heart made it all even more real.

Was it a boy? A girl? Would it look like her? Like Rick? She knew a momentary sorrow, quickly dispelled by an unexpected thought. Maybe there was a reason for this baby—a cosmic restitution for the senseless death of a promising young life. Philosophy was not her forte, and she smiled at herself.

Walking back to the campus in the spring sunshine, she felt light again, lighter than she had in days. Tulips bloomed everywhere and the old brick buildings looked beautiful and full of charm among the green of trees and bushes. A fresh breeze cleared the air, and she took in deep gulps as she walked to the history building for her last morning class. Too bad she would have to spend the next hour inside. She wished she could go to the beach and feel the sea wind on her skin and in her hair and smell the tangy scent of salt water. Next week her finals would be over and maybe one day she could

go. One day, too, she would go back to her home town
and visit the restaurant.

She had decided to go to summer school and get a
head start on her graduate studies. There were several
courses offered that she could take. There was no way
she could find a full-time job now that she was
pregnant, and she might as well do something useful
with her time. It would cost money, but it would be an
investment, and she just had to look at it that way. In
September the baby would be born, and what she
would do then she still didn't know.

Paul had been gone three days now. He had called
her every night, asking how she was and telling her
about his day. Tonight he would be back. She
couldn't help thinking about him, visualising him
sitting in a restaurant, or lying in bed in the hotel,
reading or sleeping. What kind of book was he
reading now? A mystery? Science fiction? She thought
of him touring Colorado, taking pictures of the
mountains, those magnificent snow-covered cliffs
transformed by the sun into giant glittering crystals.
Was there snow on the mountains at this time of the
year? She didn't know.

She wondered what he would say to her when he
came back. She pictured him standing in the door
again, big and tall, his piercing blue eyes sliding over
her.

There were so many voices inside her urging her to let
him in, others warning her to keep him out. So many
thoughts and feelings and fears that needed expression,
a listening ear. Was it a weakness, a lack of strength to
not be able to be sufficient to herself?

More than anything now she wished for strength, for
the courage to stand alone and do what needed to be
done, to make the right decisions. The question was
always there in the back of her mind: *What am I going
to do about the baby?* It appeared at the oddest
moments, while she was sitting in class listening to a

boring lecture or standing at the cash register in the supermarket or shelving books in the library.

Her exams, so far, had gone better than she had expected, but they weren't over yet, and she could feel the strain. Paul's appearance on the scene was ill-timed, and she could have done without the added tension. Still, she was looking forward to his return with a mixture of fear and excitement. When he arrived that evening, she opened the door to him with a pounding heart and a funny feeling in her stomach.

He was carrying a paper grocery bag with the makings of the promised meal. He put the bag on the counter, then turned to her and took her face in his hands.

'How are you both?' he asked.

Kristin swallowed. 'Fine,' she said huskily.

He kissed her gently on the mouth, and she felt a surge of longing to put her arms around him, hold him, tell him she loved him.

He released her face. 'How did your exams go this morning?'

'I think I passed. No big surprises.' She moved behind the bar and began to take the groceries out of the bag. Paul was with her in a flash.

'I'll do that. It's my turn.' He took her shoulders and propelled her out of the kitchen and into the chair in front of her desk. 'You sit and be a good girl and study while I cook dinner. I'll bring you a glass of wine to help you along.' He was grinning down at her, and she wondered if he really thought she could study with him so close.

But, amazingly, she did. Paul said not a word to her while he busied himself, making a minimum of noise. Wonderful aromas began to fill the room and she was suddenly ravenous.

Some time later he announced that dinner was served, using an exaggerated formal tone that would have done an English butler proud.

He had filled the plates and put them on the coffee table, a white candle in the middle and a glass of white wine by each plate. Kristin had bought the wine glasses the year before, cheap supermarket products that served the purpose just fine. The food was beautiful and colourful—chicken with apricots and plums, sweet green peas and white rice.

'You dazzle me with your talents,' she said, surveying the plate of food in front of her. 'It looks like a picture from a magazine with all those colours.' Then she raised her eyes to him and smiled. 'It's your profession, isn't it? Colour and contrast and composition.'

He smiled at her. 'Right.'

She saw the warmth in his eyes and suddenly the light seemed softer around them, the air lighter. It was good to have him here. It was all right, for now.

He made her go back to work afterwards, and did the dishes by himself, 'washing up', as he called it, and she managed another two hours of study while Paul sat on the couch and read the paper and later a book. He did not talk to her or disturb her in any way, and she found it was a peaceful feeling to have someone else in the room, a presence that softened the edges of loneliness.

It was almost eleven when she shut her book and put her papers away. 'I'm done.' She stood and stretched her arms above her head, then dropped them suddenly, conscious of her body, its shape and contours. She turned away—and then Paul was with her pulling her close, very close and kissing her hard. Her stomach was pressed against him and she tried to pull away, but couldn't.

'I know it's there,' he said. 'There's no need to try and hide it or be so conscious of it all the time.'

Kristin didn't reply. She stood rigid in his arms and he kissed her again, softly this time, and she could feel the weakening, the softening of her limbs. She fought against it, tightening her muscles, yet not resisting him.

He released her, saying nothing. He helped her pull out the bed before he left to go back to his motel.

The next few days were much the same. Paul would cook dinner for the two of them and stay with her for the evening while she studied. She enjoyed having him around, silent in the background, but knowing he was there. It made a difference. They were peaceful times, in a way. They talked only over dinner, quiet talk that did not touch the subject of the baby and the future. There was harmony and contentment in those evenings.

It was only Paul's departure she dreaded, his kisses and his restrained passion. Every time she fought the onslaught of her emotions, standing in his embrace with her arms hanging stiffly by her side and her hands clenched into fists.

One night he took her fists, uncurling her fingers one by one, looking into her eyes.

'Can't you relax?' he asked.

She shook her head.

'Why?'

'I don't want to. I . . . I don't want to get used to you being here.'

There was a silence. He was holding her left hand flat between his own two, his face thoughtful.

'We've got to give ourselves a chance, Kristin,' he said quietly.

With her right hand she wiped the hair off her forehead. 'It's no use,' she said, her voice lifeless.

'You can't say that. You don't know that.'

She withdrew her hand. '*I* know it, and I can say it!' She took a step backward. 'I like having you here, you know that, but it's not going to lead to anything. I can't handle it—there's too much for me to think about right now. I've got problems, and . . . and it would be better if . . . I mean, I just can't handle a relationship right now. It's all too complicated.'

'You make it complicated.'

She glared at him, 'I *make* it complicated? What do

you know about it? You have no idea at all how I feel, what it's like. . . .' She stopped, feeling oddly breathless, and closed her eyes.

'Why don't you tell me about it, then? Why don't you talk to me?'

She glanced at him bitterly. 'I'm going to have to do this on my own. I can't afford a crutch that's going to be taken away from me sooner or later. You're going back to Australia.'

'You can come with me.'

Her back stiffened. 'No!' She turned away from him. 'I don't want to discuss it any more.'

They didn't. Kristin was grateful he didn't bring it up again and she concentrated with all her strength on her finals, studying every night. Paul would read quietly, sitting in the pale circle of light from the standard lamp, an atrocity with faded blue flowers on a crinoline shade, a relic from the ancient past dug out of some dead relative's attic and considered good enough to furnish a rented room.

The exams finally over, Kristin sighed a breath of relief. To celebrate they drove out to Portland for an exotic meal at Trianon, an intimate restaurant full of lush plants and works of art.

Suddenly she had seas of time. Graduation was only weeks off, but it seemed endless. They went for long drives through the countryside, or along the scenic coastal road, taking picnic lunches assembled at the delicatessen—smoked salmon, fresh crab, French pâté, crusty breads and tropical fruit juices—guava, soursop, passion fruit and mango. She loved showing off her country to him, the beauty that was Oregon with its blue hills and rocky mountains, its green valleys and vast forests, its waterfalls and rushing streams. He carried his cameras everywhere and took endless rolls of film. She would sit on a rock, near a stream or on a needle-strewn forest floor and watch him work.

One day they drove the three hours to her home

town, arriving at lunchtime. It had been more than a year since she had last been back. Slowly they drove through the main street, past the drugstore and the dry-cleaner's and the volunteer fire department and the hardware store and the small supermarket run by a Chinese family. She had been friends with the daughter all through grade school and high school. But they had gone to different universities and lost track of each other. Where was Patricia now? Still at university? Married? Both? The past was slipping away, leaving only memories.

Kristin's stomach fluttered nervously as they neared the restaurant, built on a cliff and overlooking the Pacific. She heard the roar of the ocean, of waves breaking against the rocks. There was the familiar, salty tang of sea water and the cry of gulls soaring above.

The restaurant came into view and she held her breath for a moment. It had a fresh coat of paint, a pale pink, and she hated it on sight. It had been sea green before, with brown trim, blending in with the landscape. *Pink!* How could anybody paint a restaurant *pink*? It was abominable.

They parked the car and went inside.

Kristin took a deep breath as she looked around. The décor and the colour scheme had been changed, and everything was pink and white and frilly. Behind the cash register a strange woman in a pink blouse was helping a customer. A flashy flower arrangement, all white and pink, decorated the counter. It was so obviously fake that it made Kristin's heart cringe.

She stood there, motionless, with her heart in her throat and a pain in her chest and a whole mush of feelings of loss and sadness. She wanted to cry.

They were sitting at a corner table. How she had got there she didn't know. It felt as if she were in a trance, staring at the pale pink tablecloth. What was wrong with the red and white checks her mother had used? What was wrong with the homey country-style décor they'd had? It was warm and inviting and people had liked it. It belonged here on the rocky cliffs near the restless sea. This phoney, fussy frilliness was ridiculous. Gilt-framed pictures of pink roses on the walls, lacy curtains. It looked like a baroque boudoir, for God's sake!

Someone held out a menu to her and she took it automatically. It was new too, professionally designed by the looks of it, with ornate gold lettering on pink paper. She felt unreasonable resentment. Her eyes scanned the list of dishes offered. It was basically still the same, but the prices were higher. It offended her. Her mother had always tried to keep prices moderate and the reputation had been exactly that: Good food for reasonable prices. But prices had gone up everywhere, she admitted to herself, so why not here?

'What are you thinking?' Paul reached out to touch her hand. 'You don't look so happy.'

She shrugged, embarrassed. 'It's changed,' she said huskily. 'It's not like it used to be.'

'Of course not.' He smiled. 'Had you expected it to be?'

Kristin shook her head. 'Not really. But seeing it is different from thinking about it. And it feels bad to be a stranger here now.' She paused, looking at the door at the back of the room. *PRIVATE*, it said in gold curly letters. All her life she had gone back and forth through that door which led to the house behind the restaurant. 'I can't go through that door over there and go home. My whole life I was here, most of my memories were connected to this place, and now it feels like . . . like it's just gone, obliterated.' She stared out the window mistily, feeling childish for all those sentimental emotions. 'It's silly, I know, but I can't help it.'

'Not silly—understandable.'

Kristin looked at him with a half smile. 'One thing's the same—the view. Magnificent as ever.'

The sea, wild and turbulent, shimmered blue and

green and silver in the bright sunlight streaking down from an azure sky. White-crested waves hurled themselves against the rocks, crashing in foaming clouds of spray. Gulls flapped and dived and shrieked above the water in search of some unfortunate fish.

They ordered a big bowl of clam chowder. Clam chowder had been her mother's speciality. No way could anyone equal her in that.

'Very good,' commented Paul, perusing her face from under dark brows.

'Yes.'

'You sound reluctant,' he laughed. 'Not as good as your mother's, I'm sure.'

'It is,' she said, amazing herself. 'It's good, really good.'

His brows rose in surprise. 'Really?'

'What's so funny?'

'To tell you the truth, I thought you'd be beyond objective evaluation at the moment.'

Kristin shrugged. 'I try to be honest.' Her eyes swept the room. 'And to be honest again, I think this place looks terrrible!'

He laughed. 'Very . . . er . . . American, I'd say.'

'American? How's that?'

'All those pink frills and fake roses.'

She groaned. 'There's two hundred and twenty million of us. We don't all go for frills and fake roses.'

'True.' He tapped his head. 'Images and stereotypes and prejudices—so hard to keep under control.' His eyes gleamed with humour.

The restaurant was more than half full, the customers, by the looks of them, a mix of local lunch-timers and tourists on their way through town.

Kristin stared at the word *PRIVATE*, wondering what the people had done to the house. It had been an old house in need of considerable renovation for which there never had been any money. If she could have a look there now she would probably not recognise the place. Maybe it was just as well she couldn't walk through that door. Not knowing would keep her memories intact.

Paul gave her a thoughtful look. 'I wonder what happened to your tree house,' he said.

Kristin lifted her eyebrows in surprise. 'How do you know about my tree house?'

'You told me one night in Australia.'

She frowned. 'Oh, I remember. God, I must have bored you with my tales!' She sighed. 'I think it's probably been torn down—an eyesore, you know. You couldn't have a crude thing like that sitting in the middle of all those gorgeous roses in your pretty flower garden.'

'Now, now,' said Paul soothingly, a smile in his eyes, 'don't be bitter. Why don't you ask?'

'What they've done with the tree house? You've got to be kidding! I don't even know these people.'

'So?'

She shrugged. 'Never mind.'

'I'll do it.' He wiped his mouth, put down his napkin, strode over to the lady behind the cash register and talked to her. Kristin stared at his broad back. She heard his voice, but not his words. The woman in pink smiled, nodded, glanced across the room at Kristin, then smiled again.

Paul was back at the table. 'They sanded down the tree house and re-finished it,' he told her. 'Every weekend their two grandsons come and play in it. You're invited to go through and have a look.'

She swallowed. 'You're kidding me!'

'Absolutely not.' He took her hand. 'Let's go.'

Like she must have done thousands of times in her life, Kristin walked through the door into the living room of the house that once had been hers. It was an ordinary room with ordinary furniture and no frills or pink roses, a surprise as well as a relief. The sliding glass door was open and they walked out into the back yard—still the same back yard, the same tree house in the back, only with a fresh colour of new stain.

Memories rushed back, as Paul's arm came around her.

'It looks nice.'

'Yes.' Her voice sounded odd.

'I can see you sitting in it,' he said, 'reading a book and eating an apple. A good picture, but one I can't take.' He smiled. 'Did you have plaits?' He picked up a strand of her hair above each ear in illustration, cocking his head and narrowing his eyes as if to visualise what she would look like.

'Pigtails, you mean?' She nodded, surprised. 'Yes— long ones. How did you know?'

'I didn't know, I was just guessing. When I try to visualise you as a little girl, that's how I see you. With plaits.'

Kristin tried to picture him as a boy, but failed. 'I can't think of you as a boy at all,' she said, and he laughed.

'I was one, don't worry. I liked to climb trees and even broke a leg falling out of one once. Never had a tree house, though.'

'I'm glad mine's still there,' she said. 'I'm glad somebody is still using it.'

'Yes.' He gently turned her around and they walked back inside. They sat down again and ordered coffee and apple pie.

The lady in pink brought the dessert herself, smiling broadly at Kristin. 'Your husband told me your mother owned this restaurant before we bought it,' she remarked.

Your husband. Kristin glanced at Paul, whose face was impassive. She nodded at the woman. 'Yes. I grew up here.' She swallowed. 'Thank you for letting me see the tree house—it was very special to me. I'm glad your grandchildren play in it.'

The woman's face radiated warmth. 'You should

have seen them the first time they came here. They went wild over it!' She put the apple pie down in front of them. 'Well, enjoy your dessert.'

She would not let them pay for their meal. 'On the house,' she said, smiling. 'Come back again.'

They drove away in silence.

'I guess,' said Kristin after a while, 'if you like frills and phoney roses, you should be allowed to.'

He grinned. 'Some of the nicest people do.'

She smiled at him and felt warmth suffuse her. 'Yes.'

There were flowers from her mother and Uncle John when she graduated, and Paul was in the audience during the ceremonies. When they came back to her apartment there were more flowers. A huge bouquet of dark red roses graced the coffee table, filling the room with their perfumy fragrance. Kristin opened the card with trembling fingers.

With love, Paul, was all it said, but her throat closed up and she dared not look at him.

'Thank you,' she said, and her voice wobbled. And then she was in his arms and he held her very, very tightly, his cheek against hers.

'Will you marry me?' he said in her ear.

Her breath caught in her throat and she grew motionless with shock. She couldn't marry him, not in a hundred years. Her toes curled in her shoes and she was swept with anxiety.

'I can't, Paul.'

'Why not?'

'It's not fair to you. I'm not your responsibility. I want to deal with this myself, stand on my own two feet. I have to, don't you see?'

He shook his head slowly. 'No, I don't see. I love you. You need someone to look after you. The father of the baby is not available and I am. So why not?'

'It's not your problem and it's not your baby. Would you want me to give it up for adoption?'

'No.' Not a flicker of hesitation in his voice.

'Why not?'

'Because it's yours and you don't want to.'

'How do you know that? I haven't made any decisions.'

'I think deep down you have. I can see it in your face,' he said softly. 'Sometimes I watch you when you're just sitting, not doing anything, and I know you're thinking about the baby. There's a softness and tenderness in your face. If you really didn't want the baby you would have decided by now. You would have made arrangements.'

There was a long silence. Kristin stared at the red roses, at the shabby room, the faded carpet. Marrying Paul would be the easy way out. She loved him; he wanted her and the baby; they'd live in beautiful Sydney. But it all seemed too easy, too convenient. Something was wrong.

She knew she couldn't marry him. It wouldn't be right. It wasn't fair to Paul to burden him with someone else's child. He might regret it later, resent the child and blame her for it. She would never forgive herself.

And was it true that she had deep down already decided to keep the baby?

Sometimes, at night, she lay in terror of the unknown future, wondering if keeping the baby would be the right thing to do, wondering if it wouldn't be better to have it adopted. Other people might be better able to cope with a child, give it love and security and comfort. But lately, every time she thought of giving up the baby, everything inside her rebelled at the idea. She wanted the baby, already loved the baby. It was hers, hers alone, and no one would take it away from her.

In her head she would plan everything—a job, a baby-sitter, rearranging the apartment.

But there was always the worry. No matter how well she tried to organise her life in her head, she knew that in practice things often didn't work out according to plan. There were always the big unknown factors. What if something went wrong at the birth? What if something went wrong with the baby? How would she manage on her own? At twenty-two you didn't run back to mama like a little girl, and certainly not when she lived on another continent with a new husband.

Fear would grow into anger. She would rage at the world, at the injustice of it all. Why was it that women were always the victims? They were the ones who got pregnant, had to take care of the babies, for eighteen years or more. Their whole life was changed because of it, having to gear it towards tending to other lives.

At other times she was full of wonder at the miracle of it all. Sometimes she would lie in bed, feeling the baby move around, wondering how it would feel to hold it in her arms, and she would fill with such sweet longing it would take her breath away. Sometimes she talked to the baby—out loud or in her head—and she wondered vaguely if she were cracking up.

'Kristin?'

She gazed at him numbly.

'You do want to keep the baby, don't you?' he asked.

Her throat ached with the effort not to cry. 'Yes.' She swallowed, forcing her mouth into some sort of a smile. 'I figure,' she added with phoney brightness, 'that keeping him close is the only way I'll ever know what'll become of him . . . or her.'

And then the tears did run over and she turned away, sat down in a chair and broke down with her face in her hands.

CHAPTER SEVEN

PAUL came down on his haunches in front of the chair and put his arms around her, and leaning against the warm, solid bulk of him, Kristin let the tears flow. How long she sat there, crying noisily against his shoulder, she had no idea. Finally he lifted her chin and looked at her with tenderness and love in his eyes.

'Then why don't we just get married? That would solve everything, don't you see?' His voice was calm and soothing as if he were talking to a child. 'And if you want we can get a babysitter and you can go to the university in Sydney. I don't know how the systems differ, but we have librarians so I assume there must be a way to become one.'

'Paul . . . the baby isn't even yours!' she protested.

'It will be, won't it?'

'Is it that easy for you?'

'I've had some time now to get used to the idea.' He smiled crookedly, then very gently put his big hand on her stomach and she couldn't move away because she was trapped in the chair with him in front of it.

'Don't,' she croaked, pushing his hand away.

'Why not?' he asked gently. 'Are you ashamed of it?' She shook her head wildly. 'No!'

'Why are you always trying to hide yourself from me? Behind the breakfast bar, or by covering yourself up with the afghan on the couch?'

It was true—she'd caught herself doing it. She didn't want him to see her with her big stomach, which was ridiculous, because most of the time there was no hiding it. Paul was watching her, waiting for an answer, and she didn't have one. He took her hand and held it and she didn't pull it away.

118

'Would you feel the same if it were my baby?' he asked at last.

Kristin shook her head. 'No. It's just that ... that every time I see you looking at me I think about how it's not yours, and. ...'

'I wish it were,' he said with sudden violence. 'I wish to God it were!' He got to his feet, strode into the kitchen and poured himself a drink.

Kristin straightened in her chair. 'See? That's what I mean! It's not your baby—it can never be! You'll hate me for it for the rest of your life!'

Silence filled the room. Paul stared at her across the empty space between them.

'That is not true,' he said in carefully enunciated tones. 'That is not what I meant. I wish the baby were mine, because then you wouldn't have any reason not to marry me. For myself I don't care, at least not any more. It's not the biological process that makes you a parent in the true sense of the word—and that's been proved by thousands of adoptive parents and their children.'

'I wish I could look at it that way,' she said bleakly.

'Well, why can't you? Why can't you marry me and accept it?'

'I don't want you taking responsibility for my stupidity!' she blurted out.

Paul swung around the breakfast bar, drink in hand, and stood in front of her, looming large overhead. 'Is that what it was? Stupidity? And if so, what difference does it make now, for God's sake! I'm not exactly pure as the driven snow myself. I've committed my share of regrettable acts, and sometimes I got caught and sometimes I got lucky. It's called *life*!'

Her mouth dry, her hands trembling in her lap, her heart fluttering with nerves, Kristin glanced up at him. 'I didn't love him, you know,' she said tonelessly, and the weight of the admission filled the room and the air was heavy with it and it was suddenly difficult to breathe. 'He was my best friend, but we never . . .' she swallowed, 'we never made love except that one time. It was the night before he left and I. . . .' Her voice trailed away. How was she going to explain what had happened when she didn't even understand it herself? Why did she want to explain, anyway? Because she wanted him to understand. It seemed important that he understand. *I was lonely. I was so lonely!*

'It's not a prerequisite—love.' His voice was bland.

Kristin raised her head. 'I guess not,' she returned bitterly. 'Except I didn't think it would ever happen to me like that. I don't jump into bed with a man just for the fun of it. I . . . I was a damned *virgin*!' She looked away. She didn't want to see his face or read his eyes.

'Not a great stroke of luck,' he said softly. 'It doesn't seem fair.'

She glanced at him quickly. 'I should have known better.'

'We don't always. We're only human, no matter how experienced or intelligent we are.'

Kristin said nothing to that and he drained his glass, put it on the table and sauntered over to the window.

'I'm sorry,' she said after a pause, staring at his back.

Paul turned to face her. 'For what?'

'For everything—for letting this happen to me; for dragging you into this.'

'You didn't drag me into it. You tried to keep me out.' He lounged against the window frame, hands thrust into his pockets.

'I wish there was a way to explain it,' she sighed. 'What happened, I mean.'

'You don't owe me any explanations, Kristin. I have no right at all to know anything. And I'm not standing in judgment of you.'

Why then did she feel she had to justify herself to him, explain herself? Why then did she feel so guilty? She couldn't marry him the way she was feeling. It would always be between them. How could she ever feel right about herself if she used him as a crutch? She didn't want to feel obliged, to have to feel grateful for the rest of her life. She wanted to stand on her own two feet.

He didn't stand in judgment of her, he said. But how could he not blame her, subconsciously at least?

Misery clutched at her, a giant hand squeezing her stomach. She got up slowly. Exhaustion made her sluggish and ungainly. She heated water for some herbal tea—some magic concoction of a variety of exotic flowers and leaves and barks that was supposed to be good for frayed nerves and induce sleep. Waiting for the water to boil, she stood with her hands on her back, stretching her spine.

She made the tea. The spoon tinkled against the edge of the cup, a small sound in the silent room. Across the empty space their eyes met. Kristin took a deep breath, determined to stay cool.

'Paul . . . I don't want to seem ungrateful, but . . . but I wish you'd go home. You've been here a long time and you have a life in Sydney and a career, and . . . and I feel selfish keeping you here. I . . .' She faltered. Again the room filled with silence and the atmosphere was charged with tension.

'I am not going back to Australia.' Like bricks the words dropped into the silence. 'I am going to stay here with you, and nothing will change my mind.' The rigid stance of his body, the tautness of his muscles accentuated his words. His eyes had a deep, metallic glow.

'What about your work?' she wanted to know.

'I can do it anywhere. I found a good lab in town and I have an agreement with the owner. It'll do for a while.'

She hadn't known that.

'Besides,' he continued, 'this is a new place with different scenery and different people and it's good inspiration.'

'I hadn't thought about that.' She picked up her cup of tea from the counter and took a careful sip. It was hot. 'I know you hate this stuff. Can I get you something else?'

'I'll have another Bourbon.' At her instigation two weeks earlier Paul had tried Bourbon instead of Scotch, and now he seemed to prefer it.

I'll make a real American out of you yet,' she had taunted.

'Not a chance,' he had replied with a grin.

'Why not? What's wrong with America?'

'It's not Australia.'

Kristin poured the drink and put the glass on the table in front of him. He was sitting on the couch, leaning forward, legs apart. His forearms rested on his thighs and his hands dangled between his knees. She wondered what he was thinking as he sat there staring at the carpet.

A fly buzzed frantically against the window, half crazed by its futile attempts to break through the invisible barrier of glass. In the silent room, the sound annoyed her, and she opened the window and shooed it out. The air was hot and humid. She turned to look at Paul, running her tongue along her dry lips.

'How about if we wait a year?'

He looked up. 'A year? Why?'

'To give me time to sort myself out. I want to know I can be independent, take care of myself. I want to take control of my own life.'

'You're independent now.'

Kristin shook her head. 'I'm not. I don't *feel* I am.' Ever since she had discovered she was pregnant, she had felt adrift, not knowing what to do or where to go. The most frightening was the feeling that she had lost control over her life. It was what kept her denying her need for him. She wanted what control there was left to herself—make her own decisions, make her own life, take care of this baby who was her responsibility.

'Kristin, I don't want to wait a year.'

She swallowed. 'I need the time. Please, Paul, understand. I need the time. I need to be on my own for a while.' *Listen to me!* she said to herself. *How can I say that? I must be out of my mind. What's the matter with me?*

He looked into her eyes, slowly shaking his head. 'I think, Kristin,' he said softly, 'that you're deceiving yourself.'

Her hands curled around the cup. She lowered her gaze and stared into the pale amber tea, saying no more.

They had dinner at Kristin's favourite Mexican restaurant.

'I signed up for three classes this summer,' she said, looking up from her sour cream enchiladas. 'Did I tell you? I thought I might as well, because there won't be anything else to do and I can't work ... I mean, nobody will hire me now.' She stopped, feeling her toes curling in her shoes with tension. She had to go on with her life, even if he didn't leave. He'd just *have* to understand it. She looked with longing at his margarita. Not for her this time. Tequila and babies *in utero* did not mix. Neither did all that salt. Maybe she was reading too many articles. Maybe she could just have a sip.

'Which courses?' Paul asked evenly, studying her calmly over the salted rim of his glass.

'Beginning Cataloguing, Beginning Reference and Information Science.'

He grimaced. 'Sounds terrible to me.'

His expression made her smile. Yes, she admitted, it did sound pretty terrible, but it was necessary and she'd just have to struggle through it. Her voice sounded light and careless with relief.

'You suppose I could have a sip of your drink?' she asked. 'I know it's bad manners and all that, but I'm dying for a taste of it.'

'Have two,' he said generously, handing the glass across the table.

'Do you think I'm being silly not to have one myself? I really love margaritas, but only one and I'm half looped.'

Paul shook his head. 'Not silly at all. It's terribly potent stuff. Keep to the white wine spritzers for the time being.'

They had coffee at her apartment and listened to some records. Shortly before ten he left her, after first pulling out the bed which was becoming a nuisance because it was sticking. The next day he was back, tore the sofa apart and, with some tools borrowed from Harvey downstairs, repaired and oiled the mechanism.

'See? You need a man around the house.'

'Well, it seems I have one,' Kristin answered lightly.

The days went on like that—with a lightness and a quiet contentment and no more mention of marriage. When Paul wasn't working at the lab, they toured the countryside taking pictures. He had bought her a simple thirty-five-millimetre camera and taught her how to set the lens aperture and shutter speed. A little pocket Instamatic was all she'd ever had and she had no clue as to how to operate a manual camera.

'You think my library science courses are boring,' she challenged, 'but what about the technicalities of using a camera? This is a drag!'

He laughed. '*Touché!* I suspect it's generally true that performing the actual job is a great deal more exciting than learning the skills.'

Her first few rolls of pictures were abominable and she was horribly embarrassed, but Paul did not laugh or make disparaging remarks.

'I don't believe I have much talent in this direction,' she said with a deep sigh, looking with despair at a recent batch of pictures—over-exposed, under-exposed, shadows in all the wrong places. 'My focus is good, though. That's one thing I've got down pat.'

He laughed. 'It's simply a matter of practice.'

'When you have talent maybe it's easy.'

'Don't let anyone fool you about talent,' he told her. 'Most artists will tell you that their work takes about ten per cent talent and ninety per cent sweat and tears. It's never just easy.'

After a while Kristin could see some improvement and she was delighted out of all proportion.

Now that Paul had the use of a lab, he would bring his own prints to her apartment and show them to her, explaining what was good and what wasn't, what he had intended and what had happened. Her insight and perception grew, and she found joy in the knowledge that she had at least a grasp of what Paul dealt with in his work.

It was strange how his pictures turned out sometimes, so different from what she remembered the scene had looked like. 'It's the way I felt it,' he had explained to her once. 'It's atmosphere and mood and impression, not just the mere representation of some external reality in terms of shape and colour.'

'But how do you do it? Your camera doesn't know about what you feel. It can only record what is there.'

'You manipulate it with shutter speed and aperture settings, and with lighting. And in the lab you have control over the image on the negative in the printing process.' He waved his hand in the air, his eyes serious. 'I'm not interested in factual representation—there's nothing creative about that. My photos are visualisations of what I feel and see with my mind.'

Kristin was in awe of his work. There was something magical about his photographs, a feel, a quality she couldn't describe. They were full of life and feeling—starkly dramatic or softly subtle or fiercely passionate, evoking in her the most profound emotions. Kristin was amazed by his versatility, his sensitivity to mood and atmosphere. The printed images of his inner visions told her more about the man he was than words could ever do. She would gaze at the photographs feeling admiration and respect and a growing love.

The evenings went by, alive like the ever-changing colour patterns of a kaleidoscope—movies and dinners in intimate little restaurants, an evening of thrilling delight at the Oregon Bach Festival. He made her laugh. He made her happy. He made her forget everything but the joy of the moment. She loved him.

He bought a small second-hand car and returned the rental, a move that tasted of permanency, but Kristin made no comment. He spent much time on the phone—to Australia, to Denver, to San Francisco. The bill, which he paid, was astronomical. He talked at length to his assistant in Sydney, to art gallery managers and museum directors. By all appearances he had set up business right here in Oregon. They settled into a routine. It was almost like being married, an image she didn't have the courage to examine.

'Let's go to the beach,' he said one day, 'and go swimming.'

'I'd love to, but I have to warn you, the water is freezing. It always is.'

'I'm tough.'

'I'm not.'

Paul raised his bushy eyebrows. 'You mean to say you won't go swimming?'

'Right. Besides, I don't have a swimsuit—or at least not one that fits me at the moment.' Even if she did, she wouldn't put it on and lie on the beach with him with her stomach poking up.

'We must get you a cozzie, then.' His laughing eyes challenged her.

'A *what*?'

'A cozzie. From costume—bathing costume.'

Kristin rolled her eyes. 'Forget it. I'm not going in the water anyway. I'll wear shorts and I'll be fine, honest.'

'Let's go on Friday,' he said, dropping the subject, 'and take a picnic.'

On Friday morning he arrived bright as the day with a package in his hand. 'For you,' he said, smiling winningly and dropping the little bag in her hands.

It was a maternity swimsuit, size eight. It was a bright blue with a fine white stripe and very pretty. She looked at it, then folded it back in the bag.

'I don't want to wear it,' she said tonelessly.

'Is it the wrong size?' he asked innocently.

'You know it isn't.' She imagined him in the store looking through the rack of maternity swimsuits. A sales lady offering assistance. *May I help you, sir? A swimsuit for your wife? What is her size? Would she like something in blue?*

'How did you know my size, anyway?' she asked.

He shrugged. 'I looked at the tag in your jacket— simple. And why don't you want to wear it? Did I choose the wrong colour? Is my taste unspeakably bad?'

'I'm not going swimming,' she said stubbornly.

'But we'll be on the beach and in the sun, and it will feel much better than wearing clothes.'

She didn't reply, her eyes trained on the paper bag. It was from an expensive store; it was probably an expensive suit; the colours were right. She liked it. She hated it.

'You'll look nice in it,' Paul said quietly. 'Don't be silly, Kristin. Try it on and see how it looks.' He put an arm around her shoulders and nudged her towards the bathroom. 'Go on.'

She moved like an automaton, closed the door behind her, stripped off her clothes and put on the suit. It looked funny. At the back it was like an ordinary swimsuit, but in front it had a loose sort of skirt to cover up an expanding pregnant belly. It left nothing to the imagination. It was all out there for the world to see.

All right, all right. If he really wanted her to wear this

ridiculous thing, she would. She put her shorts and shirt on top of it and went back into the room.

'I'm ready,' she announced. 'Let's go.'

Paul was in the kitchen, taking the food they had bought the day before out of the refrigerator and arranging it in the ice chest. He straightened to look at her, closing the lid. 'Good, so am I.'

But once at the deserted beach, a secluded stretch of sand surrounded by rocky outcrops jutting into the water, she felt embarrassment take hold of her again. Paul peeled off his shorts and shirt and stretched his long body towards the sun, loosening his muscles, smiling at her. He wore short green swimming trunks, the same ones she had seen in Australia, and she knew a sudden rush of warmth in her blood at the sight of his bare brown body in the golden light of the morning sun.

He lowered his arms and put his hands on his hips and smiled at her. 'Come on, take your clothes off and let's have a swim.'

'Later. You go ahead.'

He gave her a searching look, then turned without a word and dashed off into the water. She heard his yelp as his body registered the water temperature, and she laughed out loud. Now that he wasn't there watching her it seemed easier to get out of her clothes. She lay down on a towel and closed her eyes. Paul loomed over her a moment later, dripping icy drops of water on her arms and chest, and she squealed in protest.

'I'm not staying in there by myself.' He extended a hand to help her up. 'Come with me, spoilsport.' He pulled her across the sand and there was no choice but to get in the water. It was freezing.

After only a few minutes she had had enough, and they got out and rubbed themselves dry, shivering. He poured them coffee she had brought in a Thermos, and soon the chill had gone and they lay down in the sun, feeling its warmth as a balm.

Kristin closed her eyes, absorbing the sounds of wind and water, of waves breaking against the rocks and seagulls in search of food.

'I could get used to a life of leisure real easy,' she said dreamily. 'Too bad I have to bury myself in the books again on Monday.'

Paul lay on his back, hands behind his head, squinting up at the vast blue sky. 'I can't think of anything more boring than a life of leisure,' he commented. 'Just going on from day to day and never working for anything must be deadly.' He grinned. 'Give me a good fight any day, a challenge to keep my energy flowing, mentally and physically.'

Kristin grimaced. 'Oh, my, are we being profound! I'm not up to deep thoughts today. I'm going to lie here and vegetate.'

'And I'll see if I can get some pictures of the barnacles on the rocks before the tide comes in.' He ambled off down the beach, and she watched his back, the sun shining on his smooth, muscled body. She felt weak with sudden desire and she closed her eyes.

They swam some more. They talked. They read. At noon they hungrily attacked the curried chicken salad, the ham croissants and the strawberries. Afterwards Kristin promptly fell asleep, sated with sun and food. When she awoke she peered through her lashes, seeing him next to her staring out over the sweeping length of shimmering sea. She closed her eyes again, luxuriating in the sense of peace and the smell of salt water and sun-warmed sand.

A soft, gentle touch, a hand on her belly, slowly stroking it, around and around. The warmth of it penetrated the thin material of her swimsuit and her heart suddenly thundered in her chest. Her eyes flew open and she wanted to turn away, but Paul took her arm and pulled her over on her side, up against his body. He held her tightly, pressing her into him—her breasts and stomach, every part of her touching him.

His face was close to hers, their mouths almost touching. For an endless, quivering moment they lay perfectly still, then, drawing together inexorably, their lips met in sudden, insatiable hunger. He kissed her deeply, passionately, and his mouth was hot and tasted of salt and sea. Fire raced through her blood.

'I want you,' he murmured in her ear. He kissed her again, not waiting for an answer, and his hands roamed restlessly over her back. Kristin lay still in his arms, her senses clamouring at his words, at the feeling of his body against her.

Then he withdrew slightly, letting her roll on her back. Head resting on his hand, he looked into her face, and she saw the smouldering eyes and felt her heart contract. One hand began to move over her body, slowly, sensuously, but when it rested on her stomach, she pushed it away.

'Please,' she said huskily, 'don't do that.'

'But I want to see you and touch you and feel you—all of you,' he said. 'You're beautiful, and I know you're pregnant and I want to feel it—I'd like to feel the baby move.'

She averted her face. 'No!' She felt suddenly cold.

'Don't turn away from me,' he said softly. 'Please.'

But she couldn't make herself move, and at last he lay back in the sand and was silent.

Something was wrong, and something would have to change. But in the following weeks nothing did, except that Kristin went back to classes and Paul continued to come to her apartment, cook dinner and stay with her while she studied, resuming their pre-graduation routine. Now and then during the evening she would glance at him. He would be reading a book, relaxed in his chair, left foot drawn up on to his right knee, one hand resting on his ankle. He sat so still for such long periods of time that Kristin wondered whether he never had muscle cramps. She couldn't sit still for very long herself. Every now and then she had to get up and walk around, have a drink or get a handful of raisins to chew while she worked.

Before he left at night he would kiss her and hold her, but in the end she would always draw back. She knew she was hurting him terribly, but she couldn't make herself do anything else. She wondered how long he would put up with her. There was a limit to every man's patience.

And underneath the peaceful surface of their relationship the tension grew.

Kristin had called the landlord some time ago and he had agreed to extend her lease for another year. He would send her the lease by mail, he said, as soon as he returned from his vacation in Mexico. She hadn't mentioned it to Paul. Looking around one day, she knew that if she stayed here longer she would have to make it a more cheerful place. She could start by painting the door and window frame. They were a dirty white now, and bright yellow would be an improvement. Once she had decided, she wasted no more time and bought the paint, the brushes and other necessities.

Paul found her standing on a chair, painting the top edge of the window frame. He stood in the door for a long silent moment before he entered the room and closed the door behind him.

'What the hell do you think you're doing?' he asked with barely contained anger.

Wiping the hair out of her face, Kristin gave him a bright smile. 'It's obvious, isn't it? I'm painting. I want to give this place a little sparkle I'm tired of this dump.'

'Get off the chair.' Paul's voice was dangerously calm. He held out a hand to help her down and silently she lowered herself to the floor.

'If you wanted the place painted, why didn't you tell me?'

'Why?' she asked belligerently. 'I can paint as well as the next person.'

'And your balance is lousy! You're crazy climbing on chairs like that!'

'I was perfectly safe and steady! And I'm not a cripple or an invalid.'

'No, but you *are* almost seven months pregnant!'

She maintained a stoic silence as she cleaned the paintbrush and then her hands. Then she went in the bathroom, had a shower and changed into a dress.

When she came home from class the next day, the window and the door were painted.

The following week Paul had a couple of appointments in Portland and Seattle and had to leave for a few days.

'Promise me you won't do anything dangerous,' he demanded. 'No more standing on chairs to paint or hang pictures or curtains or God knows what. Anything that needs doing can wait until I come back.'

Kristin smiled and shrugged. 'All right.'

He looked at her darkly. 'I mean it, Kristin!'

'I know. I won't, I promise.'

'I'll call you every night, about ten.'

'Checking up on the little woman, right?'

'Right.' He didn't smile.

He sounds just like a husband, she thought wryly, then smiled at him and kissed him goodbye.

Without Paul, the apartment seemed empty. Without him, sitting quietly in his chair, it was suddenly hard to study. It took an effort to concentrate. Everything seemed so meaningless.

That morning she had sat in class listening to the instructor lecturing about the life of Melvil Dewey, who, at the age of six, had organised all the food in his aunt's pantry in alphabetical order. *Do I really want to know this?* she had asked herself. *I'm pregnant. I don't know what to do. What use is dead Melvil Dewey to me?*

More and more she became absorbed by thoughts of the baby. It was moving around a lot, kicking her and sometimes keeping her awake with its antics inside her.

At times it seemed that the world at large had stopped existing, held no relevance to her life, no meaning. All the big, important happenings—social upheavals, civil wars, political assassinations, nuclear arms talks— seemed to belong to another world, alien and insignificant. What mattered now were the little things of her life—the feel of her body, the movements of the baby, the thoughts about its birth, the ongoing dialogue with it.

There were times when her worries would fade into the background and she felt serene and at peace with herself. No fear, no dread. How could she worry so? She would manage. For her baby she could do anything. She would sit quietly on the shabby blue couch, nurturing the feeling of tranquility, hands resting on her swollen abdomen. She would think about motherhood, about being responsible for another human life, a helpless bundle of life that would be totally dependent on her, and love would surge through her, and strength and determination with it. Everything would be fine. She would cope with whatever came.

The summer sales were on. Kristin found herself in the baby department of a large store and looked at all the tiny clothes in white and pale pastels. Up to now she had avoided the place, but she now felt a sudden urge to get ready, as if finally she had accepted the fact that she needed these things. She fingered the soft shirts and fuzzy blankets, wondering what she would need. In the end she bought a few shirts and two baby blankets. At home she looked at her purchases, knowing it was a small start, but feeling again the tender excitement that sometimes overwhelmed her at the thought of the baby.

It was July and the weather was turning hot. Her apartment was right under the roof and the heat was sometimes unbearable. The front window was exposed to the sun most of the afternoon and when she came home from work at the library she would open the door and a blast of heat would assault her. As she stepped inside, the air enveloped her like warm wool. The small box fan she had bought the summer before seemed to help little. She couldn't remember ever having been so hot. Maybe it had something to do with being pregnant.

The day Paul came back a thunderstorm cooled the air. She felt she could breathe again. She cleaned the apartment in a burst of energy, went grocery shopping and cooked a meal. He arrived a little after seven, and her heart leaped at the sight of him. She kissed him and held him so tight that he raised his eyebrows in surprise, smiling.

'Missed me?'

She nodded, breathless.

But later that night it went wrong again. She did not like his hands on her stomach. She was filled with anxiety and conflicting emotions, miserable because she didn't know how to deal with all the bottled-up yearning inside her. But this time he did not accept her withdrawal.

'Kristin,' he said quietly, 'we can't go on like this.'

Mutely she stared at her hands.

'Why won't you let me touch you? Why are you always resisting?'

She knew it had to come. It was unrealistic to expect he would be endlessly patient with her. Kissing alone wasn't enough. It wasn't enough for her, either, she knew that. She longed for him, ached for him. Why then did she draw back every time he touched her?

'I don't know,' she said miserably. 'I feel ... I feel funny.'

'About what? Your body?'

She nodded wordlessly.

'You needn't be,' he said softly. 'You're beautiful. You're a walking miracle. I like looking at you. I love you and I want you very much.'

She didn't dare meet his eyes. She was so selfconscious about her stomach all the time, knowing he was looking at her, seeing her with someone else's baby inside. It seemed wrong. She was painfully aware of it every time he touched her.

He was touching her now, kissing her and caressing her breasts, a size fuller now than they had been, and she could feel the treacherous longing surge through her again.

'I want you,' he whispered again. 'Don't push me away. Just relax and close your eyes.'

She tried to, she wanted to, and she lay with her eyes closed, feeling his hands undo the buttons on the front of her dress, feeling his fingers gently stroking her skin. She laid her hand on his head, sliding her fingers through his hair down to his neck, slipping them under his shirt to touch the bare skin of his back. She tried to relax, to give in to the aching longing sweeping through her.

Paul lowered his head, putting his cheek gently on the bulge of her stomach. Her breath stuck in her throat and involuntarily her hands withdrew from his back and clenched into fists. She couldn't, just couldn't. With a sob she turned on her side, away from him.

'I'm sorry,' she cried, 'I can't, I just can't!' She pulled the dress closed with fumbling fingers, hating herself, hating what she was doing to him, not being able to do anything else.

Paul said nothing. She had hurt him again, she knew. Why was she doing this? Why was she making everything so complicated? Why couldn't she just make love like she wanted more than anything else? She loved him, she loved him so much it hurt.

'I'm sorry,' she muttered. 'It isn't you—it's me. Something's wrong with me. I'm sorry.'

'Sit up, Kristin,' he said softly. 'Look at me.' He helped her up and took both her hands in his. 'Are you afraid of making love?'

She bent her head. 'I guess so.'

'It's all right, you know.' he said. 'There's no need to worry.'

'I've never made love,' she blurted out. 'Only that one time. I don't know anything. And n-n-now, with this, I—I don't know what to d-d-do.' Her throat closed up and not another sound would come. She felt so stupid, so ignorant, and tears of humiliation burned behind her eyes.

Paul wrapped her up into his arms and she knew he was laughing. She could feel the shaking of his body and she reared in fury.

'You're laughing at me!'

'I'm not,' he denied. 'Not *at* you, anyway. You see problems where none exist. It works itself out, you know. Do you think all the pregnant women of this world abstain for months on end?'

'I don't know what I think!' Of course she knew there was nothing wrong with making love. It said so in all the books about pregnancy she had been reading. It was something else, she didn't know what.

'I'm going to stay with you tonight,' he said. 'The bed is big enough for both of us, and. . . .'

'No!' She straightened her back. 'You can't!'

'Of course I can,' he said reasonably. 'I want to sleep with you and hold you in my arms and make you happy.'

'No,' she said again.

'Yes,' he said softly. 'Yes, Kristin.'

CHAPTER EIGHT

'I DON'T want to!' she said fiercely. 'I *don't*!'

Paul looked at her steadily. 'That's not true, Kristin, and you know it.' He released her and stood up, apparently not wanting to argue any further. He ambled into the kitchen and poured two glasses of wine, adding a liberal measure of soda water to hers. He lit a candle, put on some music and drew the curtains, then made her sit in the chair while he pulled out the bed, and she watched him numbly. Comfortable with his body, he moved around the room easily. Kristin liked the hard, muscled build of him. He was wearing jeans and a denim shirt with the sleeves rolled up and a wide leather belt around his waist, and he seemed to her the epitome of manhood.

He was going to stay with her and there was no way she knew to make him leave, except maybe scream and shout until somebody called the police.

She didn't want him to leave.

Yes, she did.

Her stomach felt as if she'd swallowed a load of gravel.

They sat on the bed, shoes off, drinking the wine, and Paul was smiling into her eyes. She felt feverish with his nearness, the warmth of his body and the clean, male scent of him. He kissed her nose. 'Nice nose,' he commented. Then he took her hand and with a finger drew lazy circles on her palm.

He was going to take it nice and easy, she could tell.

'Are you going to seduce me?' she asked.

'Look around you—candles, wine, soft music.'

'Not very original.'

'It's the best I could do at such short notice.'

'I thought you'd been planning this for a while.'

'Months,' he agreed affably. 'But not the details. Is it important?'

'I don't know. I've never been seduced before.'

'Well, in that case it's high time you were.'

'Are you very good at it?' she asked. 'Seducing pregnant women, I mean.'

Paul's eyes sparked laughter and he bent his head to hers. 'No,' he whispered, 'this is my first time, and I'm very nervous.'

'Ha!'

He sipped his wine, looking at her over the edge of his glass, his eyes suddenly serious. His hand closed over hers in an unconscious protective gesture.

'I love you,' he said. 'Please trust me. We don't have to make love if you don't want to. But I want to stay with you and hold you and sleep with you. I can't bear going back alone to that dreary motel room night after night, knowing you're here, alone. I want to be with you.'

'You don't want to make love?' she asked stupidly.

'Of course I want to make love. It's what I've been wanting from the day I first saw you.' He put her hand to his lips, giving her a smouldering look.

Kristin swallowed uneasily. 'I'm sorry.'

He laughed. 'You say the strangest things! Don't you want a man to want you?' His breath was warm against the palm of her hand.

'I'm ... I'm sorry I'm not very co-operative.' Why didn't he find himself a normal healthy woman who would give him a good time in bed without all this neurotic anxiety? She bit her lower lip hard. 'I'm making things difficult. You have the patience of a saint.'

There was laughter in his eyes. 'True.' The tip of his tongue touched her palm and her heart skipped a beat.

'Does that feel nice?' he whispered, holding her gaze.

She nodded, feeling warmth come into her face.

He lowered her hand and gently slid his hands up her arms and neck, then trailed his fingers through her hair, and bent his face to hers.

'And this?' He brushed his lips over her closed eyes and temples.

'Yes,' she whispered. Then she felt his lips on hers in the softest of kisses that went on for a long, long time and she began to feel all warm and shivery. Then he stopped and looked down at her smiling, leaning on his elbow.

'Did you like that?'

'You know I did.' The gravel in her stomach had magically melted away.

'Let's do it again.' But it was not the same. It was a deeply passionate kiss, and she responded to it, sliding her arms around him, hungry for more. And he didn't stop, not for a long time. When he looked up finally, eyes dark, she pulled his head down again on to her breast and he lay there quietly for some time. Her heart was beating erratically and she stroked his hair, feeling her senses clamouring.

'I can hear your heart,' Paul whispered at last. He lifted his face and put his hand over her breast. 'You feel so warm and soft. . . .' He caressed her very gently and she wished she could take off the dress because it was in the way. She sat up.

'I . . . I'll be right back.' She slid off the bed, slipped into the bathroom and caught her reflection in the mirror.

Her eyes looked big and dark, her hair was all tangled and her face was flushed. Hastily, before her courage would desert her, with leaping bounds, she took off her clothes and wrapped a robe around her, tying the belt loosely around her stomach. She glanced in the mirror again. The soft blue of the robe made her look young and girlish. She grimaced wryly at the thought, quickly pulled a brush through her hair and went back into the room. Her heart thudded wildly as she sat

down on the bed again. She felt like putting her hand
over it and forcing it to calm down. My God, she
thought, this can't be healthy!

'Drink your wine.' Paul handed her the glass and
she thought she heard a smile in his voice. She
glanced at him, but he wasn't laughing. Surely he
hadn't expected her to come back with nothing on at
all?

He was stroking her fingers while they sipped the
wine. Finally he took the glass from her and put it
down.

'Why don't you get into bed?' He stood up and
pulled back the covers. Then he turned and began to
peel off his shirt and unbuckle his belt. He had his back
to her and she slipped off the robe and slid between the
sheets. Her heart was still thumping fast, as she turned
on her side, away from him. She drew up her knees and
pushed her face into the pillow.

Moments later she felt him lie down next to her, and
held her breath. His arm came around her and she felt
his face against the back of her neck.

'Don't hide from me,' he whispered. 'Turn over,
come here.' He drew her from her side on to her back.
The sheets were cool against her skin and she felt more
naked than she had ever felt before, even though she
was covered up to her chin.

'Are you cold?' he asked.

'Yes.' She wasn't, but she didn't want the sheet
removed.

'So am I,' he said, lying too, 'let's keep each other
warm.' He hugged her close and when she felt his
warm, bare body against her, a feverish heat spread
through her. It felt so good, so good. . . . His lips closed
over hers and the lightheadedness was not just from the
unfinished glass of wine. He kissed her breasts, and the
blood throbbed in her head, but she didn't move. His
hand went down and stroked her belly, and she turned
her head, lying still, very still.

'You're beautiful,' he whispered, his hand circling around and around.

Tears squeezed from behind her closed eyelids. 'Oh, God, I wish . . . I wish. . . .' her voice broke.

'What?' he asked softly, his hands still on her belly.

'I wish I weren't pregnant. I wish I . . . I didn't feel like . . . like an overweight rhino!'

Paul laughed softly. 'I like you this way. You're more womanly now than you'll ever be. It's beautiful, I like it.'

'How can you?' she wailed.

'I just do. I like looking at you and feeling you against me, and your belly just isn't in the way, not in my head and not in my heart.' He wrapped his arms all the way around her. 'I love you, Kristin.'

'I don't understand why,' she muttered miserably. 'I'm not gorgeous or rich or particularly smart, and I'm carrying somebody else's baby.'

'None of which has anything to do with it,' he countered easily. He kissed her gently, then held her away from him a little and looked into her eyes. 'Falling in love with you was the easiest thing I've done in my life, Kristin.'

She looked at him silently. Falling in love with him had been easy too. What she felt for him she had never felt for anyone else—a sweet, magical, indescribable feeling.

'You know,' he said softly, 'when I first met you I liked you because you were quiet and unassuming and eager to take everything in around you. I enjoyed talking to you because you're fair-minded and charitable in your thinking. There's something very warm and human about you, Kristin.' He smiled and trailed his fingers through her hair.

She did not know what to say to that. She felt uneasy at this unexpected praise, and her gaze slid away from his face.

'I haven't been very lucky in the love department

lately,' Paul went on. 'I was getting tired of all those smart-alecky women who assume that every man is, by definition, a male chauvinist and put everything you say under the microscope for inspection and analysis.' He smiled wryly. 'As was pointed out to me by various females, I am not Mr Perfect, which certainly didn't come as a surprise to me, but apparently I was expected to be. I'm guilty of a variety of sins like the rest of mankind, and as far as my liberation is concerned, I can only say that I try.' He paused, frowning a little. 'I don't mind criticism. God knows I need it at times, but I can't tolerate having to justify every move I make.'

He kept on running his hand through her hair, slowly, sensuously, smiling into her eyes. 'I enjoy being with you and talking to you because I never have the feeling that you turn over every word I utter to see what's crawling beneath it. You seem to take me for what I am. With you I feel like a normal human being. With you I feel happy.'

The candle spluttered, throwing wild shadows across the room. In Australia Kristin remembered wishing she was more sophisticated, more interesting company. She had wondered why he seemed to enjoy talking to her. Now she knew, and she felt aglow with warm, sweet delight.

She smiled at him. 'Because I'm one of those uncritical females from an earlier age who sit at your feet and admire your superiority and take every word you say for gospel truth.'

'Oh, no. If you were you'd have married me weeks ago, safe and secure.'

'It's not that easy any more.' She looked at him. 'I do know a chauvinist when I hear one, though, and I've never heard you say anything I interpreted as blatantly chauvinistic or prejudiced.'

'Because you weren't looking for it. You're not so damned paranoid about it.' Paul kissed her lightly. 'And what I noticed,' he continued softly, 'was that you never blamed or accused the father of your baby, although certainly he carried part of the responsibility for preventing a pregnancy.'

'I was equally responsible,' insisted Kristin.

'It would have been very easy to accuse him, just the same.'

Accuse Rick of what? Nothing she couldn't accuse herself of as well. But she didn't want to think about that now. She let out a sigh and closed her eyes.

Paul's fingers began to trail a path down her nose and chin and neck. Peace and languor stole over her, until suddenly she was wide awake as the baby jabbed a little limb into her abdominal wall.

Her eyes caught Paul's gaze directed at her stomach. 'My God,' he whispered in astonishment, 'it kicked you!' His hand settled softly on the spot and, as if in answer, the baby kicked again. Her heart swelled at the look of wondrous delight in his face. 'I felt it!' he said, as if it were the most miraculous thing that had ever happened to him. 'I can't believe it! It felt so strong! It must be a boy, a football player!'

She laughed, looking at him mistily. 'Did you hear yourself? *Did you hear yourself?* That ... that was a sexist remark!'

He grinned. 'I know—I couldn't help myself.' He buried his face between her breasts and held her so close she could barely breathe. They lay there quietly for a long time and she could feel his love and his need for her. Finally he raised his head and kissed her gently. 'I love you,' he muttered.

I love you, too. Kristin longed to say the words, but they wouldn't come. Her throat was dry and refused to make the sounds. *I can't do it,* she thought miserably. *I can't go through with this.* A whole complexity of reasons and emotions twirled and twisted, until she knew only bewilderment and an aching sadness that brought tears to her eyes. Oh, damn, she thought, I don't want to cry. What's wrong with me anyway? All this weepiness is driving me nuts!

'What's wrong?' asked Paul softly.

She shook her head. 'I don't know.' Her body was rigid with the effort not to cry. She knew he had to feel it, too.

'I won't hurt you, Kristin, I promise.'

She swallowed. 'I know.'

'I'll just hold you.'

Her face against his shoulder, she lay still for endless minutes until finally she could feel herself relax again. He raised his head and kissed her cheek, her temple, her ear.

'Close your eyes and go to sleep,' he said softly.

Kristin opened her eyes wide. 'I thought. . . .' Her voice trailed away and she swallowed at the constriction in her throat.

'This was only the first instalment of the Great Seduction,' he said solemnly. 'More is yet to come. Just be patient.'

'It's not fair to you,' she whispered awkwardly, and he laughed.

'I'll take a cold shower! I'll survive.' He leaped out of bed and disappeared in the bathroom. Huddling under the sheet, Kristin stared at the door. *Why does he put up with me?* she wondered. *It's ridiculous. Why doesn't he just go back to Australia and forget about me? I'm no good to him at all.*

Never in her life had she thought it would be like this. She had never expected lovemaking would create all this anxiety and selfconsciousness on her part. But then she had never expected to be pregnant before she had met the man she loved.

There was no way she could fall asleep now; it was still early and she was too keyed up. She slipped out of bed and put her robe back on. She needed something—tea, orange juice, hot chocolate. Hot chocolate with marshmallows.

Barefoot, she stood in the kitchen stirring the hot milk into the chocolate when Paul appeared next to her, a towel wrapped around his waist. Leaning over her shoulder, he peered into the cup. His skin felt cold.

'You're cold,' she said.

'That was the whole idea,' he grinned. 'What are you doing? Hot chocolate? Was our session that traumatic?'

'I don't understand you,' she gulped. 'How can you stand here and joke about it?'

'What else can I do?'

'Why aren't you mad at me?' Kristin kept her eyes determinedly on the mug of chocolate. She felt like a spiteful wife. *Not tonight, dear. I'm too tired and I have a headache.*

'I don't *feel* angry.'

'I'm no good to you,' she muttered miserably. 'Something's wrong with me—I'm not normal.'

'There's nothing wrong with you—nothing that a little time and patience won't take care of. I'm not worried about it.' He sounded perfectly confident. He stood behind her, moving her hair aside with one hand. He kissed the back of her neck, his lips firm and warm against her skin. 'Make me one of those too,' he whispered in her ear.

'A hot chocolate?'

'With marshmallows.'

'I thought you'd rather have Bourbon,' she commented.

'There's a time for everything. This is the time for hot chocolate.'

Kristin took her mug with her to bed, but she kept her robe on. Paul sat in the chair, feet up on the foot of the bed and began to tell her a funny story about the time he had been on assignment in a remote outback region in Queensland to take pictures of the Aboriginal people.

Only a short while ago he had wanted to make love to her, and now, cool as could be, he was telling her a story. *He doesn't mind*, she thought in amazement. *He seems perfectly content just sitting here talking to me, drinking hot chocolate.*

She hadn't seen any Aboriginal people when she

was in Australia, and he told her that most of them lived in the tropical north and mostly kept to themselves. He told her what he knew about their culture, a culture rich with fantasy and myths. Kristin listened with fascination to stories about a weeping opal, a rainbow serpent, and a burning anthill, about the capture of fire, the origin of the platypus and the birth of the butterflies—stories full of colour and magic and imagery, and she was enthralled.

She watched Paul as he talked, relaxed in his chair, dark forearms resting on his thighs, and the warmth of love and gratitude spread through her. She closed her eyes. After a while she began to feel drowsy with the heat of the milk and the rich, soothing tones of his voice. He swung his feet down and took both their mugs and put them in the sink. Quickly, while his back was turned, Kristin slipped out of the robe and between the sheets.

Paul turned, smiling at her with glints of humour in his eyes. 'Sleepy?'

She nodded, burrowing under the covers.

'I'll read for a while,' he said. 'Will the light bother you?'

'No, I don't think so.' She really was tired now.

He came over to the bed and put his hand on her cheek. 'Go to sleep,' he said softly, and she nodded, her eyes already closing, and fleetingly she felt his lips brushing hers. She felt herself slipping away, secure in the knowledge that he was there in her room, reading quietly, and wouldn't go away. He would stay here with her tonight.

Later she awoke, and she did not know how long she had been sleeping or what time it was, Paul was next to her in the bed, eyes closed and sound asleep. He was lying on his back, the covers pulled up halfway across his chest. Raising herself on her elbow, Kristin looked down on his face. His features were relaxed. It was a good face, not handsome, but strong and masculine with its square chin and bushy eyebrows. She longed to run her finger over the scar on his cheek and feel the texture of his skin, but she did not want to wake him up. Or did she?

Looking at him filled her with sweet, clamouring sensations. She wanted to feel him close again, feel his hands on her body. She wanted him to make love to her. How could she have turned him away? She loved him; he loved her. She wanted him, longed for him. Even the thought of making love was enough to make her heart race, and she lay back quietly, staring into the dark. *Next time I'm not going to act like a neurotic*, she vowed.

At long last she fell asleep again. Paul had not stirred.

He was holding her when she awoke and he was kissing her eyes. She lay still, and his mouth moved to her cheeks and nose and lips. Still groggy with sleep, she stirred and moved against him, feeling warm delight suffuse her. He looked up and smiled into her face.

'See how nice it is to wake up together?' he whispered, trailing his lips down her chin and neck. His hand reached down and cupped her breast. 'Mmm, still there,' he murmured.

Then, unexpectedly, he let go of her and got out of bed. 'Time to get up. Shall I start the coffee?' He wrapped a towel around his waist and took off for the kitchen, smiling at her across the breakfast bar. When he wasn't looking Kristin came out from under the covers and quickly wrapped the robe around her. She made the bed, still warm from their bodies, and when she was ready to push it in, he called out to her to stop it.

'I'll do it.'

'I can do it. It goes easily enough since you oiled it.'

He was next to her, pushing in the bed. 'While I'm here there's no need for you to do it.'

She had to smile. 'It won't hurt me, you know,' she said gently, and he grinned at her.

'I need to feel useful,' he said lightly. 'I want to pretend you need me.'

There was a silence and their eyes locked and the room shivered with sudden tension. Paul's smile had faded and she knew what he wanted her to say, but the words wouldn't come. She swallowed, glancing away.

She didn't want to become dependent on him. She didn't want to need him. She needed to make her own life, prove to herself she could take care of herself, live with the consequences of her actions.

'You've done a lot for me already,' she said at last, a catch in her voice. She glanced at him and he smiled faintly, but it didn't reach his eyes. She felt wretched, and it didn't make sense, because what she wanted to say was, *I love you. Please love me. Please take care of me and my baby*, and that was what he wanted to hear, but she couldn't make herself say it.

Paul made coffee, peeled her a grapefruit and fixed some breakfast. He talked to her as if nothing had happened, but it was there between them, no matter how he pretended it wasn't. She tasted nothing. The scrambled eggs might have been candlewax, and for all she knew the coffee could have been liquid shoe polish.

It was Thursday, and she had no classes and no work shift at the library. An entire day all to herself. She had an appointment to have her hair cut and afterwards she planned to go shopping for a dress. Paul took his cameras and took off on what he called a 'hunting trip', after he had first dropped her off at the hairdresser.

She sat in the chair and had her hair washed, brooding over their relationship.

It was not normal; it was not normal at all.

The girl massaged her scalp. She was a fluttery thing of about sixteen, apparently a trainee, and she devoted herself with great concentration to Kristin's head. It was a good feeling and she was beginning to relax, realising how tense she had been until then.

'Would you like a conditioner?' the girl asked in an

exaggerated girlish tone. Kristin looked at her in the mirror. She could do with one herself—her hair was bleached and looked dry and brittle—not good advertising for the beauty salon! But when you were in the throes of puberty you liked experimenting to try and find a more glamourous you. Kristin remembered only too well her own experiments and how awful she had looked. It hadn't been so many years ago. Why then did she feel so old?

'Yes, please.'

The girl massaged the rich creamy mixture into her hair. Kristin wondered if any would penetrate her skin. She had read somewhere that fifty per cent of many cosmetics applied to the skin ended up in the bloodstream—not an appealing idea. She wondered about the baby. She wished she hadn't agreed to have the conditioner. Oh, God, she thought, I'm getting paranoid! No more aspirins, no more sugary foods, no more alcohol except an occasional glass of wine diluted with soda water. Easy on the caffeine, on the starches. . . . Danger lurked in every corner. She was afraid of small children with spots, of cats and raw meat: rubella, toxoplasmosis. There was no end to her fears, real or imaginary. She sighed involuntarily.

Later she sat in front of the mirror and looked at herself while the hair-stylist combed her hair. In the bright light her face looked pale, and with her hair wet and moved away from her face, she looked like a sallow potato. She had never liked the way she looked in the beauty shop—something to do with the light, maybe.

'I just need it trimmed a little—an inch or so.' It had been quite a while since she'd last had her hair cut; she had never had the time. She had felt so rushed lately, afraid to run out of time before finals, before the baby was born, before she didn't know what.

The stylist's name was Jane, according to a tag on her peachy pink smock. She was fortyish, had dyed black hair that hung past her shoulders, a too-red mouth and a toothy smile. Kristin knew her from previous visits to the beauty salon. She separated Kristin's hair in sections and put clips in to keep them out of the way. 'When is the baby due?' she asked conversationally.

'September sixteen.' Kristin stared straight into the mirror.

'Is it your first?'

Kristin nodded, wondering if she would have to spend the next twenty minutes or so making gushy small talk about babies. She didn't want to. Not like this, anonymously, meaninglessly.

The women lifted up a strand of hair, slid it between her fingers and raised her brows at Kristin. About an inch was sticking up, ready to be snipped off. 'Is this right?'

'Fine.'

'Would you like a boy or a girl?' asked Jane, snipping away busily now.

'It doesn't matter to me. Either is fine.' It seemed a minor point in view of the big issue of survival.

'As long as it's healthy, that's what I always say,' Jane volunteered. 'I have two, you know, a girl and a boy. It worked out nicely, but I wouldn't have cared what I had. But men, they like a son, they always do. Does your husband want a boy?'

'He doesn't care either way.' When you were pregnant people assumed you had a husband, she'd found that out a while ago. The assistants in the doctor's office called her Mrs Henderson in front of the other patients, although it was stated plainly in her file that she was not married. It was done out of consideration for her, a courtesy not really necessary in this day and age, but she had not objected.

Sometimes she wondered what would have happened if Rick hadn't been killed. Would he have suggested that they get married? She couldn't imagine being married to him. She couldn't imagine Rick as a married man. She visualised him as the eternal bachelor with too many women around him to be able to make up his mind about one.

The woman kept on talking while she snipped away inches of hair. 'How's this?' she asked at last. 'Short enough?'

'It's fine.'

She picked up the hair-dryer and began to brush and blow-dry Kristin's hair. Ten minutes later Kristin had paid and was out the door, hair shining and smoothly hanging down to her shoulders.

In the department store she found the maternity section and searched through the racks for a dress. She felt awkward being here, as if somehow she had no right or did not belong. It irritated her that she should feel this way, but she couldn't shake it off.

She needed something cool and loose. She had only two other dresses and jeans were beginning to be too warm most of the time. There were several she liked, and she hung them over her arm and went into the fitting rooms.

The blue one with the white dots was too sweet and girlish and made her look like an overgrown Shirley Temple. The other one was a pretty stripe, white and pink and lavender, and she stared in the mirror, thinking she actually looked nice—feminine, even a little elegant, if you could be with a pregnant belly out front. It was an expensive dress, at least compared to what she usually spent on her clothes, but it was on sale and affordable. She decided to take it.

She wanted to look beautiful, to feel beautiful. Suddenly she couldn't wait to get out of the store, go home, put on the dress and wait for Paul. She wasn't sure what time he would be back. When he went on one of his solitary trips anything could happen to keep him busy working.

Kristin spent the afternoon making a hearty chef's salad for dinner with lots of cold chicken, ham and cheese. She hummed as she worked, chopping up chicken and onion and green peppers, slicing tomato and cucumber and cheese. She delighted in the colours and the crispness of the lettuce, cool against her fingers, as she arranged everything in an attractive pattern on a large platter. Stepping back, she surveyed her composition with a critical eye, then smiled at herself. It was worthy of a picture in a magazine. Paul would be proud of her. In a spurt of creativity she mixed up her own dressing with oil and lemon juice and an adventurous mixture of herbs and spices.

At four all was done and ready and she realised she was tired. She lay down on the couch with a book and a cup of herbal tea, another magic brew that was supposed to stimulate and refresh, and promptly fell asleep.

CHAPTER NINE

A BRIGHT flash of light awoke her and she opened her eyes to find Paul in the room with a camera in his hand. He looked dishevelled, his jeans dusty and his sneakers muddy. It looked as if he had been crawling through the woods. He probably had.

He grinned. 'Sorry, but the temptation was too great.'

'You took my picture?'

'Right.'

Kristin sat up and ran her hand over her belly, straightening the dress. 'Not fair, with me not knowing!'

'If you knew you wouldn't let me. You looked very peaceful, and very pregnant.'

'Thanks,' she said with a grimace.

'Do you mind that I take pictures of you now and then?'

She shrugged. 'As long as you show them to me before you do anything with them.' She wasn't eager to find herself hanging in an art gallery one day in all her bulbous glory.

Paul laughed. 'I couldn't do anything with them without your permission. You'd need to sign a model's release before I could sell them.'

'Oh, I see. I hadn't thought of that.'

'Also,' he said blandly, 'you could charge me a fee for posing.'

Kristin batted her lashes at him. 'For you I work for free.' She came slowly to her feet and gave a moan. She felt so sluggish. She stretched her spine, wondering if her body really was supposed to be built to carry around all that extra weight. 'Don't you dare take a picture now!' she threatened.

'I wouldn't dream of it,' he lied, straightfaced. 'But you do look very sexy in that dress.'

'*Sexy?* You've got to be kidding.'

Laughter shone in his eyes. 'It's all in the eye of the beholder, isn't it?'

'You've got some very weird eyes.' She hid a yawn behind her hand. 'What time is it?' Her watch was in the kitchen where she had taken it off to wash the vegetables.

'Almost six.'

'I slept for *two* hours?'

'Don't ask me. I was out in the big bad world working.'

It was then that she noticed the suitcases by the door. Her heart nearly stopped. Was he leaving? Her mouth went dry.

'Why are your suitcases here?'

He looked at her steadily. 'I'm moving in,' he said calmly.

It took a moment to gather her wits. 'You can't,' she said then. 'It's impossible!'

'Why?'

'The place is too small! And . . . and besides, we . . . we can't go on this way. I mean, in September. . . .'

'There's a solution. We can get married and find a bigger apartment. And after the baby is born we'll go back to Australia.' He seemed unperturbed.

She swallowed. 'No, Paul, no! I've told you—I've got to do this on my own.'

'Then I'll stay here.' There was finality in his tone. 'I don't like you living here alone.'

'I'm not! Emma and Harvey are downstairs. I can call on them if I need help.'

'Last week I found you standing on a chair painting a window, for God's sake!' he said roughly.

'You're not responsible for me!'

'You keep saying that.' There was a hint of bitterness in his voice and she felt instant remorse.

Kristin took a deep breath. 'Can't we please let it be? Can't we wait for a year? Next year, I'll come to Australia and . . . and we can see how we feel then.' She was aware of the pleading in her voice.

His brows drew together in frustration. 'I know how I feel now, dammit! If I'm going to marry you, I want to do it now! If I'm going to be the father of the baby I want to be there from the beginning!'

Tears burned behind her eyes. 'Don't you yell at me!'

'You frustrate the hell out of me!'

'Then go home and leave me alone!' Tears were running down her face and she turned and stumbled into the bathroom, slamming the door. She lowered the toilet cover and sat down, sobbing. The door opened and Paul came in, pulled her up into his arms and held her. He smelled like sun and dust and crushed grass.

'I'm sorry,' he said in her ear. 'Please don't cry.'

'I hate it!' she sobbed. 'I hate fighting! I can't stand it!'

'I'm sorry I lost my temper.' He kissed her wet cheeks, her trembling mouth. 'I worry about you,' he said huskily.

'I know, I know.' She put her arms around him and rested her face against his chest.

They ate the salad and had fresh peaches for dessert, and later they went to a movie. Paul held her hand all through the movie. They had a drink at a piano bar afterwards and it was late when they finally came back to the apartment.

Taking her nightgown into the bathroom with her, Kristin got ready for bed. She was nervous. She lay in bed waiting for him and he came out of the bathroom, wearing nothing, and slid next to her in the bed. He turned out the light and the room was dark.

He came over to her and took her in his arms. 'Why are you wearing a nightgown?' he whispered.

'I always wear one.'

'Not when you're sleeping with me.' He slid it off her shoulders, down to her belly, knees and feet. She lay still, feeling his hands as they moved down her body, taking the nightgown and tossing it on the floor.

'Hey!' she protested. 'I paid good money for that!'

'A serious mistake. Never spend money on night-clothes if you want to keep a man happy.'

It was a warm night. The windows were open, but there was not much of a breeze. Even the sheet she had covered herself with was too warm.

'Do we really need that sheet?' asked Paul.

'Yes.'

'I even turned the light out for you. I promise you I won't see a thing. I'll even close my eyes, if you insist.'

'You're making fun of me.'

'Never!' But he was laughing, and then he began to kiss her, first teasingly, then more seriously, murmuring sweet nothings in between. His hands caressed her with expertise and a feverish tension began to spread through her. Her breathing quickened and she felt warm, so warm. Slowly he removed the sheet and she hardly noticed, didn't care any more. Her senses heightened, her hands moved over his body, touching, exploring, and she marvelled at the feel and the strength of it.

Something was changing. Paul's kisses were no longer soft and gentle, but filled with a fiery need that wouldn't be easily denied. She loved him, she wanted him. No time now for objections, for guilt or worries. No matter what would happen they would have this night. She had a floating sensation, as if her body was weightless, free of the earthly bonds of time and place. There was only the man she loved and the yearning and urgency that made them cling together breathlessly. Arms, legs, hands and mouths, all were touching, stroking, searching.

Kristin shifted slightly in an effort to move closer still

and she felt the rapid beating of his heart as her hand touched his chest.

His breathing was shallow and he raised his head to look at her in the shadowed darkness of the room. 'Kristin?' His voice was soft as a caress.

'Paul . . .' she whispered, 'Oh, Paul. . . .' She wanted him, needed him, and there was no consciousness of anything else, nothing but the wonder of their bodies. And he had done this to her, teaching her there was nothing more glorious than their bodies, nothing more beautiful than the loving they shared.

He moved her slightly, carefully, and he was close, so close, and with a gentleness more loving than anything she had ever known they blended together. Again he whispered her name. There was a spiralling of delight, a soaring of the senses until the mutual tension broke into shivering waves of relief.

She lay still, her heart throbbing, and tears ran down her face—strange tears of joy and relief and peace and love. 'I'm sorry,' she whispered, 'I don't know why I'm crying.'

He kissed her eyes. 'I didn't hurt you, did I?' he asked, and she shook her head, smiling tremulously. His face, so close to hers, was the most beautiful face she had ever seen. Deep, tender feelings came welling up as she looked into his eyes, but there were no words she knew that would tell him what she felt. She closed her eyes and her lips sought his. They kissed softly, gently, desire sated, and his hand rested lightly on her belly, and it was good.

It was hard to concentrate on her work the next day. Paul was constantly in her thoughts, and she barely heard a word as she sat in class listening to a boring lecture on the history of librarianship and librarians. What had ever possessed her to enter this course of studies?

'What is this all about?' Paul asked her that evening

when she sat poring over a book about cataloguing. He was leaning over her shoulder and looking at her book. He'd just come out of the shower and he smelled of soap and shampoo and his hair was still damp. His breath fanned her cheek and she knew a sudden headiness at his nearness.

'I'm learning how to classify books and magazines and journals, etcetera, etcetera, and how to give them a code so we can find them on the shelves.'

He shook his head in dismay. 'Well, to each his own.'

'It's sort of interesting. Dull, but interesting.'

'You're full of logic tonight, I can tell.'

'It's hot in here. I can't ever remember being so hot all the time. It's scrambling my brain.'

'I'll mix you a nice cool drink.'

Kristin caught the glitter in his eyes, and she felt breathless with the need to hold him and feel him close to her again.

'No alcohol,' she reminded him.

'Haven't you studied long enough? It's after ten.' He stood behind her chair and put his hands on her shoulders, sliding them down to cover her breasts. 'Let's go to bed.' His fingers gently rubbed her nipples through the fabric of her dress, and she closed her eyes against a wave of dizzy desire.

'I'm not tired,' she whispered.

'It's better that way.'

Kristin fought for composure. It was embarrassing; she was practically melting in her chair. She sighed, pretending reluctance. 'Oh, well, I guess I'll quit for tonight.' She closed the book and put her notes away. His hands moved away from her breasts.

'Don't tell me my competition is a book on cataloguing,' said Paul in an injured tone.

She came to her feet, turned and put her arms around him. 'Not too much,' she whispered in his ear.

She stood in the shower covering herself in clouds of perfumed soap and watched the bubbles streaming away down her belly. She dried quickly, brushed her teeth and ran a brush through her hair. Her eyes glittered strangely. My God, she thought, look at me—wanton and willing! Then she smiled. Maybe I'm normal after all, she reflected.

She slid into her robe and entered the room. The bed was pulled out and Paul lay stretched out and naked on the sheet, hands behind his head. Her heart lurched at the sight of him. She averted her eyes and he laughed softly.

'Do I embarrass you?'

'You could have covered yourself up!' she protested.

'Why? To hide from you? I don't want to hide from you, Kristin.'

She looked back at him, keeping her eyes determinedly on his mouth. 'At heart I'm a prude, you know.'

He nodded gravely. 'So I noticed. Fortunately, it's curable. Come here.' He reached out his arms to her and she moved forward, standing still by the side of the bed.

'Take off your robe,' he said softly, loosening the belt for her. She slid it off her shoulders and let it drop to the floor. He moved aside and drew her down next to him. He switched off the bedside lamp and they lay in the silver moonlight that streamed through the open window on to the bed.

'I love you,' he whispered, his eyes a deep, inky blue. He stroked her hair. 'It's a miracle I've kept my sanity through these last months. I think of you, look at you and all I want is to hold you and make love to you.' His face moved closer, his mouth almost touching hers. She moved slightly, searching, and their lips came together in urgent longing.

Paul made love to her with gentleness and skill. His mouth and fingers searched the warm, soft places of her body, rousing her to heights of delight she had never thought possible.

Later, after he had drifted off to sleep, draped against her back, hands on her breast, Kristin lay staring into the shadowed room, feeling sadness invade her. Like a living presence it had been waiting in some dark corner of the room, yanking her back to reality in the stillness of the night when no voice, no noise disrupted her thoughts.

Love, marriage, baby. To Paul everything was so simple. To her it was a jungle of conflicts, and all she had was herself to lead her through. Making love had not changed that.

The next day he came home, carrying several books. 'I spent the afternoon at the library,' he announced, dropping the books on the coffee table.

Kristina raised her brows. 'Where? Downtown?' Without special permission he wouldn't be allowed into the university library.

He nodded. 'In that massive piece of ancient brick.'

She laughed. 'In Oregon nothing is ancient. We can barely lay claim to anything antique. What did you do in the library?'

'I've been reading up on pregnancy and childbirth,' he said evenly, 'and I brought some more to read.' He lowered his frame on to the couch, stretched out his legs and folded his hands behind his head.

Kristin swallowed. 'Why?'

'Why do you think? I want to know. I've never had a reason to find out about the finer details of this adventure, and now I do.'

She was silent. A feeling, delicate and fragile, spiralled upward and her throat closed. She gazed at the desk, saying nothing.

'I understand,' he went on calmly, 'that natural childbirth is *de rigueur* these days. Have you decided what you want?'

She swallowed at the lump in her throat. 'Natural childbirth requires classes, Lamaze or something, and you need a husband.'

'Wrong. You need a *coach*. Nobody says you have to be married.'

She stared at him. 'What do you mean?'

Paul got to his feet, drew her out of the chair and over to the couch. He gave her a steady look. 'If you want natural childbirth and if you want to go to Lamaze classes, I'll be your coach.'

For a moment she couldn't speak. Her vision blurred. 'You want to be there when the baby is born? Why?' she asked huskily. She wasn't his wife and it wasn't his baby.

'Because you need someone and I happen to love you and because I want to.'

Kristin blinked furiously, but still the tears ran down her cheeks and she averted her face so he wouldn't see. He saw anyway. He turned her face towards him and kissed her softly.

'Kristin,' he said quietly, 'why don't we just get married? It'll make everything so much easier.'

She shook her head. 'No. Please, let's not talk about it any more, Paul,' she said thickly. She bent her head to avoid his eyes.

He came to his feet without replying and went into the kitchen. She heard him opening the refrigerator and then the sounds of pots and pans. He was making dinner. She had hurt him again. She leaned her head back and closed her eyes. I'm so tired, she thought. I'm so tired of everything.

She hadn't wanted to encourage him. But there he was, living in her apartment, sharing her life. If only he'd wait for her, give her time.

The next day she found the lease in the mail, sent to her to sign and return to the landlord. As she read through it quickly, the breath suddenly caught in her throat, then her eyes flew over the lines again. *No children, no pets*. Clear in black and white. It was not a new stipulation, she realised. It had been in the lease all along, but she'd never given it any thought before. The lease was exactly the same as it had been last year, and the only change was an expected increase in rent.

She sank heavily into a chair, staring at the paper, feeling panic rise inside. She would have to find another place—soon. She willed herself to stay calm. This was not the only apartment in town; there were others. Certainly she should be able to find another one?

A thought occurred to her. What if she called him, asked him if he'd make an exception for her? Only for a year.

Her hands were clammy as she dialled the number. His wife answered the telephone. A moment later the landlord himself was on the line. As calmly as she could Kristin explained her situation. Could she please have the apartment for one more year? She was angry to hear the quiver in her voice.

He was sorry, he said politely, but no exceptions. He had trouble before—complaints about noise, crying babies. He hoped she would understand.

She hung up the receiver, restraining herself so as not to slam it down. She took a deep breath, trying to calm herself.

Paul sensed her preoccupation that night. 'Is something wrong?' he asked.

Kristin shook her head numbly, pretending to study. He did not persist. He did not make love to her that night, but he held her close until she drifted into a restless sleep.

Without telling him, she started the search the next day. Dead tired, she came home, having looked at four different apartments without success. Landlords were not interested in renting a studio apartment to an unmarried mother, and proper apartments in apartment buildings were too expensive.

Over dinner Paul gave her a searching look. 'What's wrong, Kristin?' he asked.

'Nothing.' She pushed her food around on the plate,

avoiding his eyes. She felt so dejected that she could barely keep from bursting into tears.

'You look exhausted. Are you all right?' There was concern in his voice.

'I'm fine.' She took a bite of the pork chop and chewed it, feeling revulsion. She had no appetite whatsoever. She put her knife and fork down and pushed the plate away from her.

'When is your next doctor's appointment?' he asked. 'Friday?'

'Yes. And for God's sake don't fuss over me!' she snapped. 'I'm fine. I'm just not hungry, and I'm tired.' She slid off the stool and waddled into the bathroom and locked the door. It was the only place she had any privacy any more. The apartment was too small for two people; it was getting on her nerves. Paul's suitcases were in the way; his clothes were in the way; his damn toothbrush was in the way! She glared angrily at the blue brush in the glass next to hers as she lowered herself on the toilet cover. Taking deep breaths she tried to keep from bursting into tears.

After a few minutes she got up, washed her hands and face and brushed her hair. She stared at herself in the mirror. She had the colour of overcooked noodles and there were circles under her eyes. She put on some blusher and lipstick.

There was a short rap on the door. 'Kristin?'

She unlocked the door and faced him. He eyed her intently.

'I want to know what's wrong,' he said shortly.

She took a deep breath. She might as well just tell him. 'I have to find another apartment. I can't stay here after the baby is born—it's in the lease. I went out to look for another place this afternoon, but I didn't find anything.'

'So that's why you're so tired,' he said flatly. 'You've been out looking for flats.'

Kristin said nothing.

'Why didn't you tell me?'

She felt tight with tension. 'It's not your problem, Paul.'

She knew he was angry then. It emanated from him in great waves. His jaws were clamped shut and the silence thundered in her ears. Then he turned, walked out the door and closed it quietly but firmly behind him.

CHAPTER TEN

WITH trembling legs Kristin sank into a chair. She'd really done it now. This was it—Paul had had enough.

The silence surrounded her, stifled her. She looked around the empty room. A pair of his sandals lay near the couch. The paper he had been reading lay spread out on the coffee table. He would come back, of course. His things were here, his cameras. . . . She knew a momentary panic at the thought of never seeing him again.

Well, that's what I wanted, didn't I? I wanted him to leave.

Her hands clenched and unclenched, her feet were twitchy, she couldn't sit still. She struggled to her feet. Standing in front of the window, she stared outside, seeing her life projected into the future. No Paul, only herself and the baby, somewhere in an apartment like this with a view of patched roofs and small yards cluttered with toys and lines full of washing, of weathered porches with sleeping cats and broken windows covered with plastic. Alone with a baby. Work, classes, no money, no love. No Paul to talk with, to hold her and love her.

She was seized with terror. What if he didn't come back tonight? What if he came for his luggage tomorrow while she was in class? If he didn't come back tonight she would stay home tomorrow and wait for him.

What if she married him? He would be the father of her baby—only he wasn't. He would have the responsibility for the rest of his life. Maybe he would start to resent her, stop loving her. The thought alone was terrifying. How was she going to live with herself knowing she had done that to him? Knowing too that she hadn't had the strength to stand on her own two feet and make her own life.

Sooner or later she would have to do without him. Leaning on someone for support was always a temptation when you were down and alone. Marrying him would be so easy. Kristin turned away from the window. In the kitchen she took out a box of raisins and shook some out. She ate them absently, gazing blankly at the stove top.

The baby wriggled and turned around inside her. Not long from now she would be a mother—but even now it was still difficult to perceive herself in that role. Her life would be filled with the details of baby care—feedings, diaper rash, unexplained crying, fevers, wakeful nights. She would have to worry about the babysitter and whether she would take care of the baby properly. Would she let it cry and not pick it up? Would she hold and hug it enough? Oh, the luxury of staying at home and taking care of your baby yourself. . . .

She put the box of raisins back in the cupboard.

When the baby grew up she would have to tell him or her something. Already she could hear the questions: *Where's my daddy? Why don't I have a daddy like everybody else?*

She walked over to the chair and lowered herself down with care and put her feet up on a footstool. She felt like an old woman. She looked down on her distended abdomen. Would it ever be flat again? It seemed incredible that it should. It was unbelievable that her body could stretch out to these gargantuan proportions.

There was a knock on her door, and with a groan she heaved herself out of the chair again and went to answer it. It was Emma, long-legged in very brief shorts and a bright red skimpy top, clutching a huge catalogue to her chest.

'Hi, how are you?' she asked, smiling brightly.

Next to all this cheerful slenderness, Kristin felt like a dour elephant. 'Fine, thanks. Come on in.'

Emma dropped the catalogue on the coffee table and sat down. 'Were you studying? I don't want to bother you. . . .'

'No, no, you're not. Would you like a cup of coffee?' Please say yes, she pleaded silently. I need some company.

Emma hesitated. 'Yes, please.' Suddenly she seemed a little uneasy, and Kristin wondered why.

'I thought you'd be gone for the summer,' Kristin said, pouring hot water into the filter cone.

Emma grimaced. 'I wish, I wish. Harvey can't get away. He's writing his thesis and he's determined to have it done by Christmas, so he's working like a maniac day and night. He's unbearable, and he's driving me up the wall! I told him if we can't get away at least for a week, I'll go by myself. I need a change now and then.'

The coffee ready, Kristin put the mugs down on the table and sat down across from Emma. 'What's the catalogue for?'

Emma looked uncomfortable. She flicked her long dark hair back over her shoulder with her left hand, and the small diamond on her ring caught the light and shot tiny sparks across the room. 'I hope you don't mind me prying, but . . . er . . . oh hell, how do I say this delicately?'

'Don't worry about it.'

'All right.' She took a deep breath. 'Are you planning to keep the baby?'

Kristin stared at her. She couldn't for the world imagine what it had to do with the Sears catalogue. She nodded. 'Yes.'

'Oh.' Emma looked relieved. 'You see, my sister has a baby cot she doesn't need any more. Her youngest is too big for it now and she was telling me over the phone the other day that she's getting rid of her baby things, and—well, I thought of you. All that stuff is so expensive and I thought I'd ask you if you wanted it.' She gave Kristin a questioning look.

Kristin stirred her coffee. 'I don't have a cot yet. I . . . I really haven't bought very much at all yet.' It was getting to be high time to do something about it. What if the baby came early?

There was a short silence. 'I know this isn't any of my business,' Emma said uneasily, 'but I keep thinking about you, and how you're going to manage, and about that man who came to get you at the party—is he staying with you?'

Kristin nodded. 'Yes.' She knew the unspoken question, and she knew too that it was more concern than curiosity that made Emma ask, 'He's not the father. He's the son of my mother's new husband.' She paused and stared at the cup in her hands. 'He's only staying for a while.' *He may be leaving tomorrow*, she added silently.

'Are you going to stay here after the baby is born?'

'I wanted to. I asked the landlord if I could have the place for another year and he sent me the lease, and when I read it I realised that he doesn't want any children or pets. I've looked for something else this afternoon, but I haven't found anything yet.' She smiled brightly, not wanting Emma to know how desperate she felt. 'Maybe I'll get lucky soon, and if not, there's always the Salvation Army.'

'Did you ask him if he wouldn't make an exception?'

'Yes. I got a very polite refusal.'

'The bastard!'

'He's concerned about the noise, he said. And really, generally speaking, this is no place for kids or pets—no outside, not even a balcony. I mean, they'd tear the place down in a matter of weeks.' Why am I defending him? Kristin wondered.

'A baby won't! And besides, this is a dump already. It took us weeks to get our place habitable and he didn't want to pay a cent.'

'The rent isn't very high, compared to other places.'

'True.' Emma looked around. 'I see you painted the door and the window frame. Looks nice. Too bad somebody else is going to enjoy your efforts.' She grimaced regretfully and put down her coffee cup. Then she reached for the catalogue, opened it where a piece of paper marked the place and turned it for Kristin to see. 'About the cot—it's one like this. My sister says it's in good condition and it has a good mattress to go with it.'

Kristin looked at the picture. It was a simple white cot, with some pretty transfers on the foot end. 'I like it. What does she want for it?'

'Twenty dollars, with the mattress.'

'That isn't very much.'

'She doesn't need the money. She just likes to see somebody use it instead of putting it in the attic where it's no good to anyone.' Emma smiled. 'Shall I tell her you want it? They live in Roseburg, but they're coming here this weekend for my birthday and they can deliver it right to your door.' She hesitated. 'And . . . and if the money is a problem, don't worry about it. Any time is fine.'

There was a lump in Kristin's throat. 'Thanks,' she said and her voice shook.

It didn't occur to her until after Emma had left that the cot could have been saved for Emma herself. She and Harvey had been married for three years now and within the next year or so both of them would have their doctors' degrees. It wouldn't be unreasonable to assume that they would have a baby in the next couple of years. Maybe that was why Emma's sister had mentioned it to her in the first place.

It was after ten and Paul had not returned. Kristin tried to concentrate on her work, but her thoughts kept drifting and her fears kept surfacing. She struggled her way through several chapters on various reference works—encyclopaedias, statistical books, almanacs, atlases, bibliographies, government documents, and she sat staring blindly at the assignment in her notebook. Which reference works would most likely provide the answers to the following questions? Which is the longest bridge in China? The most expensive place to live in South America? The tallest Texan? The smallest river in Europe?

Who cares? she thought in a flash of fury. It was absurd. Here she was wondering about the longest bridge in China while her life was falling apart at the seams. She slammed her books closed, took a shower and went to bed. But sleep eluded her. Even in just a few days she had become used to having Paul next to her, to feel the presence of another person, to the warmth of his sleeping body next to her. It was impossible to sleep, and she lay staring at the ceiling, listening for the sound of a car outside. It was normally a quiet street and whenever she heard a car approaching, she held her breath, but no car stopped.

It was only just after eleven, but it seemed a lifetime, when she finally heard him come home. What if he came to pick up his things now? Quietly he let himself in, took off his clothes in the dark and disappeared into the bathroom. Relief flooded her, then the old anxiety returned. The shower made splashing sounds and ten minutes later Paul came back into the room, soft-footed, and slid noiselessly between the sheets. He thought she was asleep. Or maybe he knew she was awake but wanted to avoid a confrontation. Maybe he didn't care.

Kristin lay rigidly on her side, her back turned to him. She would never go to sleep like this, with this anger between them. There was such a heaviness inside her, a load of regret and sorrow she knew not how to assuage.

What if she turned and told him she was sorry—sorry for what? For hurting him, yes. But she had no strength now for an argument. She just wanted to go to sleep knowing he was no longer angry with her. Slowly she turned on her back, then on to her other side. He was lying on his back, eyes closed, but she knew he wasn't asleep. Carefully she put her hand on his chest, feeling the solid beat of his heart—and then his hand came up and covered hers with the slightest of pressures. It was as if a weight rolled off her and relief brought tears to her eyes.

After a moment he turned towards her and held her gently, saying not a word, and they fell asleep without speaking.

The smell of coffee and frying bacon greeted her when she woke up. Paul was in the kitchen, bare-chested, wearing only jeans, and waving a spatula around. For a few moments Kristin watched him unobserved, love rising inside her on a warm tide. Then he noticed her looking at him and grinned.

'Hungry?'

'Yeah.' She yawned, and looked at the clock. 'But I don't have much time. I have an early class today.' She groaned. 'Reference.' She hadn't done her assignment.

'Better hurry, then. Come and sit down and eat this, it's ready.' He took the coffee pot and poured some for her while she got out of bed and put on her robe.

With some effort she climbed on to one of the stools at the breakfast bar. She didn't like feeling so awkward and moving so clumsily, but Paul never made any comment about it, as if he knew she could not bear being teased about that. Anything was fair game, but not her pregnancy.

He put the plate in front of her and sat down himself with a cup of coffee.

'What about your breakfast?' she asked.

'I'll have it later. You eat first and get ready.'

He wouldn't mention yesterday, she knew. She ate her toast, eyeing him surreptitiously.

'What are you doing today?' she asked.

'I have work to do at the lab. I'll be there most of the day, I expect.'

As she waited for the college bus Kristin wondered what Paul's plans were. Would he stay until the baby was born? If she didn't marry him he couldn't stay here forever, could he? Eventually he would have to go back to Australia and his work over there. It was outrageous the way he had disrupted his life and career because of her. It couldn't go on. She did not need his protection. She was hardly the first unmarried mother who had had to manage on her own.

Yet the thought of him leaving was so devastating, she couldn't bear to think about it. But if she didn't marry him he would leave. It was a simple truth. Oh, God, she thought, I'm going crazy. Why can't I make up my mind?

The bus chuggalugged up the hill and came to a shuddering stop in front of her. She hoisted herself up the steps and sat down near the exit. Sitting on the bus with the other students made her feel old and grown-up. They all seemed to her so young, so careless, so without worry, even though she knew it wasn't necessarily so. She glanced at the girl across from her. Skin-tight designer jeans, a T-shirt, long straight hair, gold hoops in her ears and no make-up on the calm face with the clear grey eyes. Not a worry in the world, or so it seemed. But appearances were deceptive, Kristin knew. A myriad problems could be hidden behind that calm exterior.

Kristin was free at eleven and for ten minutes she examined the notices on the board in the student union. Offers for sale of cars and typewriters and tents and cameras. Offers to type term papers and theses. Job offers of various kinds—grocery delivery, camp guide for teenagers, tutoring. ... It went on and on. There were no new apartments for rent, and looking over the list she saw little that looked promising—she had checked out the best yesterday. It was a hopeless situation, unless she decided to spend a considerably higher amount of money for rent, and to do that frightened her; her financial situation was too shaky. For a few months she could manage, but she didn't know what kind of job she would be able to find after the baby was born.

As she stood there, staring dejectedly at the board, Vanessa appeared at her side, dressed in black jeans and a deep pink silky blouse, looking thin and elegant.

'Hi. What are you looking for?'

'An apartment. I can't stay in mine after the baby is born,' said Kristin matter-of-factly.

'Oh, great. The way we don't get discriminated against—it makes me sick.'

'Doesn't make me feel too good, either,' she returned dryly, 'but try and fight it when you're almost eight months pregnant. Besides, a man with a child wouldn't be able to stay either, I assume.' Kristin wasn't eager to listen to another one of Vanessa's tirades about women and discrimination and she hoped this would nip it in the bud. What bothered her about women like Vanessa was their across-the-board generalisations. She had no patience for that. It simply wasn't true that *all* men were the same, that they *all* wanted only one thing, that they were *all* male chauvinists.

Vanessa shrugged reluctantly. 'I suppose you're right. Have you had any luck finding something else?'

'None whatsoever. Landlords and landladies don't like unmarried mothers.'

'Have you thought of putting up a notice yourself? Or placing an ad in the paper?' queried Vanessa.

'That's an idea. I've got to do something.'

Vanessa frowned, as if in thought. 'You know, I just remembered something. I know a couple with a kid and they're moving out soon because he finished his Master's and they're leaving.' She hesitated. 'It's not a great place and it's on the other side of town, but. . . .'

A small spark of hope dispelled some of Kristin's depression. 'I'd try anything. It won't hurt looking.'

'I don't know that it's free,' Vanessa warned, 'but I'll call. How about right now?'

'Would you? Really?'

'Sure.'

They found the phone and the number, but the phone kept ringing and ringing and no one answered.

'Oh, hell!' Vanessa slammed the receiver down. 'Sorry. We'll try later. How about a cup of coffee? My treat—I need to get off my feet.'

While they had coffee and a cheese sandwich, they composed an ad for the notice board in the Students' Union and one for the local paper. Later Vanessa tried the number again, but still there was no answer. She promised to keep trying. 'I'll call you when I know something.'

After lunch Kristin went to the library. She had no more classes that day, but she was due at three for a couple of hours' work. She found a quiet corner and worked on a book review until it was time.

She was no longer climbing ladders to shelve books, but she was kept busy typing cards, checking for overdue books, and keeping her fellow students from stealing books, tearing out pages or pictures or smoking pot in the stacks. Policing was not a job she relished, but it was a necessary evil. She had once found a large, expensive art book stripped of several of its photographs; presumably they were now gracing the walls of some student pad. The lack of respect some people had for the property of others always amazed her.

When she came home after work, Paul was cleaning lenses and filters, all his paraphernalia spread out on the breakfast bar. There was no cooking in evidence.

He suggested they sample a Lebanese restaurant Kristin had mentioned once, a small place started by some Lebanese students a few months before. They had taken over a cheap hotdog and hamburger joint and transformed it with some gaudy Eastern decorations and great food. The menu was limited—homus, baba ghanoush, kibbeh, stuffed vine leaves, lamb kebabs and rice with pine nuts, and a few more dishes, all of them delicious. Within weeks the place was packed with students almost every night.

They were lucky to find a table for two. There was still the same furniture—formica tables and plastic-covered chairs, but the atmosphere was nice and it didn't seem to matter. The Lebanese students themselves served the food and stopped to talk and explain about the food when time allowed.

'It's good, isn't it?' asked Kristin as she ate the kebabs with relish.

'Mmm,' Paul agreed, his mouth full. His eyes were smiling at her. Was yesterday forgotten? Not to be mentioned again? What was he thinking behind those smiling eyes? She looked away and watched the people at the other tables.

It was funny that Paul didn't seem out of place here, even though he was older than most of the clientele. His easy manner and his casual clothes made him fit into most places, and for some strange reason it pleased her.

They finished the meal with strong, syrupy Arab coffee and small pieces of rich pakhlava dripping with butter and honey.

'This is terrible,' groaned Kristin. 'Tomorrow I have to see the doctor again, and he'll yell at me for gaining too much weight.'

Paul paid for the meal and they left the restaurant. He opened the car door and she struggled in while he watched her with a straight face, trying not to laugh. Well, it isn't funny, she thought belligerently. He should try it some time!

'I want to show you something,' he said after he had slid behind the wheel and started the engine. They drove slowly out of the street, turning right instead of left.

'Where are we going?' she asked.

'Wait and see.'

It wasn't long until she realised what he had in mind.
They stopped in front of a large apartment building.
Kristin followed him to the elevators without a word
and a few minutes later they stood in front of a brown
wooden door and Paul produced a key to open it.

It was a beautiful apartment, fully furnished.
Stomach muscles tensed, jaws clamped together, Kristin
walked around, surveying the large living room, the two
bedrooms and the modern kitchen.

'Whose is this?' she asked stiffly.

'It belongs to a Mr Harrison. He's away on business
in South America at the moment.'

'How come you have the key?'

'I rented the place for three months.'

'For *three* months? Who rents out his apartment for
that short a time?'

Paul shrugged. 'Harrison.'

'How did you get it?'

He sat down on one of the comfortable chairs and
stretched out his legs as if he was ready to settle in. 'I
went to an agency this afternoon and I was lucky.'

Kristin felt an unreasonable bitterness. *He* had no
problem getting what he wanted. All he did was walk
into the door of some agency and hey presto, it was
done.

'Do you like it?' he asked casually. 'It's not too far
from the campus—there's a bus at the end of the street.
And we can move in over the weekend.'

Her heart was thundering in her chest. She swallowed
hard. 'Paul, I can't move in here. I need a place of my
own, with a long-term lease.'

His expression did not change. He came to his feet
and strode to the door. 'We'll talk about it at home.'

They drove back to her apartment in a nerve-racking
silence. It was an effort to walk up the stairs and she
had to stop several times. By the time she made it to the
top she was out of breath.

She sank into a chair while Paul heated water for tea.

The phone rang, and she reached out and picked up the receiver. 'Hello?'

'Kristin? This is Vanessa. I ran into Joan an hour ago—you know, she's the one living in the apartment I was talking about.'

'Yes, yes.' Her heart was suddenly beating rapidly. 'What did she say?'

'They're leaving at the end of August. As far as they know the landlord hasn't rented it out again, because no one has come to see it yet.'

'How big is it?' asked Kristin. 'Did you ask?'

'A living room, a bathroom, a kitchen and one bedroom. The baby slept with them.'

'A lot bigger than what I have now.'

'I've got the landlord's phone number here. Why don't you just call him? You have a pen?'

Kristin wrote down the number on the edge of the newspaper. She was uncomfortably aware of Paul's presence. No doubt he realised the general trend of this conversation. She felt a stab of guilt.

'I wonder if I could come and see the place,' she said into the phone. 'I suppose I could give her a call and ask if she'd mind.'

'I'm sure she won't. Let me give you her number too.'

Kristin scribbled it down. 'Thanks a lot, Vanessa.'

'You're welcome. I hope it's what you want.'

Kristin said goodbye and replaced the receiver. She tore off the piece of newspaper with the numbers. It was a relief to know it was too late to call now. She didn't want to call while Paul was around. She'd wait until tomorrow.

He placed a cup of tea in front of her on the table, his face impassive. He sat back on the couch saying nothing.

Kristin sipped the tea. It was too hot. She wished he would say something, but she had the feeling he was waiting for her to open the conversation.

'You must hate me,' she said into the silence. 'I'm

sorry, I really am. I know you mean well, but ...
but I want to do what's right. I want to take care
of myself, Paul. I can't just expect others to take
responsibility. . . .'

'You've said it all before,' he interrupted. 'I just don't
accept it.'

'It's true!' she flared.

'Kristin, you keep coming up with excuses. First, you
didn't want to "burden" me with someone else's baby.
Then you decided you wanted to be independent. It all
sounds very commendable, but something's wrong.'

'I don't know what you mean. They're not excuses.
They're *reasons*! That's different.'

'I don't understand what you're trying to prove,
Kristin. There's no doubt in my mind that you could do
it all—have the baby, bring it up alone, hold down a
job and get a degree. You could do it all. But you'd
deprive the baby of a father and you wouldn't have my
love.' He paused fractionally. 'The question is, how
happy would you be?'

Her mind produced no answers. She twisted a strand
of hair around her finger, her head bent.

'Tell me one thing,' he said quietly, 'and please tell
me the truth. Do you love me?'

Her heart began to pound painfully. She swallowed,
then nodded. 'You know I do,' she said huskily.

'I do? How do I know that? You've never told me.'
His voice was laced with bitterness, and she cringed at
the look in his eyes.

It was true; she had never told him.

She averted her eyes. 'I'm sorry.'

'You're *sorry*?' he exploded. 'Tell me, how long are you
going to punish yourself? You love me, but you want
me to leave you alone, so you can take charge of your
own life, have your baby, bring it up alone. Are you
going to marry someone else later on? Or are you
sacrificing yourself all the way down the line until
you're old and grey? Do you want to play the martyr?

Poor abused woman, giving up love and life for one mistake—if you want to call it that.' He stopped, and the air around them shivered with his anger.

Kristin jerked upright in her chair and stared at him in horror. She had never seen him like that, so passionately angry. The shock of his words rippled through her and she felt like protesting, defending herself, but her throat was closed. He was towering over her like some avenging god, spewing fire and she shrank from him in fear. She couldn't speak, paralysed with the impact of his outrage.

'You know what's the matter with you?' he continued fiercely. 'You feel *guilty*! You don't want to marry me because you feel *guilty*! For some strange reason you feel you have no right to happiness and you're *punishing* yourself by rejecting marriage to me!' Anger leaped like fire in his eyes, and she stared at him, stricken.

She wanted to hear no more. She couldn't stand it— she had to get away. Without a word she got up and walked out of the door. She stood at the top of the stairs looking down into the darkness. Her legs were trembling so badly she knew she would never make it down in one piece. Now and then you would hear about some desperate woman throwing herself down the stairs. She shivered at the thought. Slowly she lowered herself to the floor and sat down at the top of the stairs, leaning her head sideways against the wall. *Guilty, guilty, guilty*—the word seemed to echo through the empty stairwell. *Guilty, guilty, guilty.*

The door opened and Paul was standing next to her.

'Go away,' she croaked.

'Come inside, Kristin.'

'No—I'm staying right here. I'm comfortable here and I don't want to hear any more. I've had enough, you hear? Enough!'

He took her arm. 'I'm sorry I lost my temper. Come along, we'll talk about it.'

She wrenched her arm free. 'No! I don't want to talk

about it! And I'm not coming in until you're gone! You have your own place now, so why don't you just leave me alone?'

'I'm not leaving. Suit yourself.' He turned and strode back into the apartment.

Ten minutes later Kristin was still sitting at the top of the stairs and beginning to feel slightly ridiculous. She didn't want to go back inside, but she'd have to go somewhere. Fatigue made her muscles feel like butter. Emma would take her in, but where could she sleep? The couch wasn't fit to sit on, so sleeping there was out of the question. In her condition an air mattress on the floor was not desirable. Sleeping these days was enough of a problem already. She was beginning to feel like a refugee, evacuated from her residence without a place to go. A good picture she'd make now, sitting here with her big belly in this dismal stairwell. Just the thing for the Sunday newspapers!

The door opened again and Paul came out with two fresh cups of tea. He sat down next to her on the steps and handed her one. She didn't take it. 'I don't want it,' she muttered.

Unperturbed, he put it down near the door.

He's like a rock, she thought suddenly. Immovable. He won't go, he won't leave. Her mind produced an image of the sea and the waves breaking on the rocks. Paul, immovable in the middle of the tumultuous sea of her life. Nothing she said or did would make any difference. Her objections and arguments and resistance had no impact on him, were like the frenzied waves crashing futilely into the rocks, dissolving into clouds of powerless spume.

He sipped his tea and looked at her, and she couldn't look away. There was no anger in his eyes now, only love and sadness. Her throat ached with misery.

Guilty! Again the word reverberated in her mind. *Guilty, Guilty.* . . . Something broke inside her and great heaving sobs shuddered through her body. Paul held her, saying nothing, and his arms around her were like a haven.

Guilty. Guilty because she hadn't loved Rick. Guilty because she could never tell her child that she'd loved his father. Guilty, guilty, guilty. For all those months the guilt had flourished like a hidden weed, undetected, secretly strangling the life out of her.

Had she unconsciously rejected Paul as a self-imposed punishment? Had her mind supplied all those convenient excuses of self-sufficiency and independence to cover up the guilt?

'It's true, you know . . . I'm . . . I'm g-guilty. Look what . . . what happened to me!' She took a shuddering breath, her face buried against his shoulder. 'I was stupid, s-s-so *stupid*!'

'Not stupid. Just human, like the rest of us.'

'I didn't love him. I don't even have that for an excuse.' Her voice sounded strange on her own ears, bitter, anguished. 'How could I have ever done that? How? Why? When I didn't even love him?'

'It happened—it just happened, Kristin.'

Something stirred inside her, a memory. *It happened—it just happened*. Those words had been hers, spoken a lifetime ago. Her mind produced a picture of Rick and the remorse in his eyes. Tears came anew and she wept bitterly, not caring now, only overcome with the need to let it all out.

'Kristin, he was your *friend*. That counts for something. You loved him as a friend. Friendship is essential in our lives, a valuable, elemental emotion.'

'You don't *sleep* with your friends,' she wept.

'It happened once, Kristin. *Once*! Who knows our deepest needs? Our most hidden motivations? We all do things we don't understand later. I don't mean that to sound as some profound wisdom of my own, but it's true. What you did was no crime, Kristin. You're twenty-two years old and this isn't the eighteenth century. You can't spend the rest of your life doing penance. You have the right to love and happiness, like everyone else.'

She bit her lip. 'You really think I was denying you to punish myself?' Her voice was thick with tears.

Paul grinned. 'I'm not a pyschologist, but it certainly seemed to me like it.'

'I must have a warped mind.'

'Do I look like somebody who'd love a woman with a warped mind?'

She smiled tremulously. 'I guess not.'

He stroked her hair. 'I love you like I've never loved anyone, Kristin. I love the baby, I *want* the baby. And all I wish is for you to accept it, not to feel guilty, not to feel that the baby is in the way, because it's not.' He released her suddenly and got to his feet, reaching out a hand to help her up. 'Come, I have something to show you.'

They sat down on the couch and he handed her a large folder. There were photographs inside—twenty, twenty-five maybe. And they were all of her.

Slowly she looked at them, one after the other, feeling a stillness grow inside her, a breathlessness and a wondrous excitement.

They were not like any photographs she had ever seen. They were beautiful and fascinating, with a strange, mystical quality. Although she was looking at herself, she barely recognised herself in some of them. In all of them she was obviously pregnant, but with changing expressions—sad, happy, thoughtful, excited, angry, tired, lively—her feelings always clear in her eyes and face. They were all hauntingly beautiful, tender, delicate, and taken with obvious love. In a flash of insight she knew that no one but Paul could have taken these pictures, no one could have perceived her the way these pictures showed her. And it was not only a matter of technique and expertise. It was love—love for her and love for her body and for the baby inside.

There was a great welling up of emotion, a sweetness, a warmth that filled her and brought tears to her eyes.

The pictures told her more than any words could ever do. Paul loved her and the baby, and he would never resent it. To him the baby was a miracle, not one that he had created, but a miracle in its own right. It was there in the photos, clearer than words.

And then she could see no more, because the tears blinded her, brimmed over and slowly rolled down her cheeks. She moved the photos aside so as not to spoil them and raised her face to his.

She reached out her hand and he took it and sat down next to her. She smiled through her tears.

'They're beautiful,' she said huskily.

'It's how I see you,' he said softly. 'It's how you make me feel.'

'I don't understand it.'

'You don't have to. I just want you to believe it.'

'Yes.' She looked at his face and his eyes dark with love and tenderness, and she was swept with heart-soaring relief.

'I love you,' she whispered, and the words flowed easily, naturally. 'I'm so glad you stayed with me. I'm so glad you didn't leave me.'

CHAPTER ELEVEN

THEY were married in the office of the Justice of the Peace, a formality without much ceremony. Only Emma and Harvey attended the wedding. Kristin had bought a new dress for the occasion, but she hardly looked like a bride in the pale green affair with its wide skirt draped over her belly. She didn't care. Nothing mattered but the love and peace that had permeated every part of her being.

The lack of ceremony didn't seem to bother Paul in the least. Neither did he seem put off by the curious looks of the Justice, who was obviously wondering why they had waited till the very last moment.

Paul was in the best of moods, his eyes smiling at her all the time.

'He's crazy about you,' whispered Emma after it was over, then laughed selfconsciously. 'Oh, God, what a thing to say to a bride! As if there should be any question!'

Flowers and telegrams had arrived from Australia, from her mother and Uncle John, and from Scott. It had taken her a week of agonising before she had written a finished letter to her mother telling her about the baby, about marrying Paul, about coming back to Sydney soon after the baby was born. A letter had come back filled with a mixture of astonishment, worry, love, acceptance and congratulations. Paul had found Kristin dripping tears on the paper.

They went for a honeymoon weekend to a small, out of the way hotel. There were flowers and champagne in the room and they had dinner on the candlelit terrace that had a view of green valleys and wooded hills. The air was fragrant with the scents of pine and sun-drying hay.

She stood in the shower, soaping herself, when he knocked on the door and came in. She peeped around the shower curtain, seeing his smile, and her heart leaped.

'I thought you might want your back washed,' he said.

She stared at him, startled.

'I'll join you in there,' he decided, stripping off his clothes and leaving them on the floor. 'Water conservation, you know.'

'You can't!' she protested.

His mouth quirked. 'You keep saying that. I can and I will. I married you, didn't I? Doesn't that prove anything?' He moved the curtain aside and stepped in.

They stood in the streaming water, arms around each other, and he kissed her wet face. He took the soap and lathered up his hands, refusing the wash-cloth, and ran his hands all over her in smooth soft strokes, looking into her eyes all the while. Kristin began to move her own soapy hands down his body and for timeless moments they touched each other with heady delight.

Her legs grew weak. 'I . . . can't stand any more,' she murmured. 'You said something about . . . water conservation?'

Paul dried her off with a huge white towel and carried her to the bed, lifting her as if she weighed nothing at all. He stood by the bed, dripping water on the carpet, and began to dry himself before he joined her on the bed.

'My hair is all wet,' she muttered, as he began to kiss her.

'So is mine,' he whispered, 'do you mind?'

'No.'

He kissed the tips of her fingers, one by one, softly, sensuously, his blue eyes sparkling merriment. He liked to take his time over the preliminaries, playing, teasing, a sweet, wonderful kind of torture.

'I've never done this before,' he whispered a little later. His mouth and hands were doing wonderful things to her body.

'Done what?' she said breathlessly. She was floating, drifting, intoxicated by the heat of his body, the feel, the clean masculine scent of it. Her hands on his chest registered the heavy pounding of his heart.

'Made love to my wife. I like it.' His eyes were full of tenderness and warmth and her heart swelled with love. Drawing his face to hers, she searched for his mouth.

'I hope you'll still like it twenty years from now,' she whispered against his lips.

'You can count on it. It's going to get better and better all the time.' He put his face between her breasts and she stroked his hair.

'I didn't know it could,' she murmured.

Paul laughed softly. 'Oh, it can. You just wait, my love, you just wait!'

And then there were no more words. He made love to her in the most tenderly passionate way and she was caught up in the rapture of the moment, the colour and warmth and euphoria of loving.

She had never seen Paul happier. And as the days went on, she could feel herself grow happier too, more cheerful and relaxed. She began to feel comfortable with herself, with him. They talked about the future, about going back to Sydney. Laughter came so easily these days, it amazed her. She felt like a different person.

It was a joy to live in the new apartment. Together they bought the necessary things for the baby, and she was touched by Paul's interest in everything that concerned the baby. The cot from Emma's sister stood ready in the bedroom, but as it turned out she would only be using it for a few weeks before leaving for Australia.

Paul did not go to Denver for the opening of his

exhibition, despite all Kristin's protests that she would be all right for one night. He was staying close, he said, and nothing could change his mind. Having discovered the truth of that, she stopped arguing.

They went to Lamaze classes together. Kristin was the biggest one in the class and felt terribly selfconscious in the beginning. But seeing the other women, looking equally funny lying on the floor with their bellies poking up and doing breathing exercises, she began to relax.

'I have to register at the hospital,' she said to Paul one evening, feeling her heart pound in sudden fear.

He looked up from his paper, frowning. 'Don't you do that when you're admitted?'

She ran her tongue over her dry lips. 'Yes, usually. Only with pregnancy they like you to do it ahead of time so you don't have to worry about it while you're in the throes of labour.'

'All right, we'll go tomorrow.'

The next day she stared at the forms given to her by the desk clerk, frozen for a moment. One for the hospital admittance, one for the birth certificate. *Mother's name, place and date of birth, address, religion. Father's name, place and date of birth. . . .*

Paul put a pen in her nerveless fingers. 'You fill in your part, and then I'll do mine.'

Kristin's hands were trembling when she filled in the required information, then she slid pen and paper over to Paul. He wrote quickly in large, bold letters, signing his name thickly at the bottom.

They were silent until they had left the parking lot.

'Do you think it was illegal, what we did?' she asked, and her voice sounded strange in her ears.

He shrugged. 'I have no idea. I don't expect anyone will ever challenge it.'

'I love you, you know,' she said, and there was a catch in her throat. He took one hand off the steering wheel and squeezed hers.

The last weeks went by so slowly. Kristin slept in short stretches, unable to get comfortable, feeling more awkward than ever. Paul was patience itself, the very epitome of a loving husband.

The baby announced itself in the middle of the night, and with amazing cool, Paul took charge and drove her to the hospital. All through her labour Paul was there, helping her, reassuring her. He did not grow white or faint or do any of the things men were supposed to be doing. The baby was born at six minutes past one in the afternoon—a healthy boy, wrinkled and red and crying lustily.

Paul's hand squeezed hers hard. 'You did well,' he said huskily.

Kristin was so relieved it was over, she cried and laughed at the same time. The baby was laid carefully on her stomach. Her hands came up and touched his tiny face, and from nowhere the words came in soft sounds and calming murmurs, and the crying stopped.

She looked at Paul in amazement. 'He stopped crying,' she whispered. 'I talked to him and he stopped!'

Some time later, after she had been wheeled back to her room and dozed for a while, they brought her something to eat. She was ravenous, and suddenly flooded with a peculiar sense of elation. She began to talk and she couldn't make herself stop, while Paul, sitting by her side, listened with patient humour in his eyes.

The baby was brought in, washed and dressed, and she held him close against her body, looking down at his tiny face, examining the little fingers and toes. The eyes were closed and the tiny mouth puckered and made sucking noises. She felt a surge of blind, all-encompassing love, and tears came to her eyes. *He's a miracle,* she thought in wonder, *he really is.*

She glanced up at Paul. He was gazing intently at the two of them and love welled up in great waves, liquid, flowing, filling every part of her.

'Paul?' Her voice quivered. 'Would you like to hold him?'

Light sprang in his eyes and he came swiftly to his feet, reaching out his hands in eager anticipation.

He was waiting, she thought. *He didn't want to ask.*

'Go to Daddy,' she whispered, handing the warm, soft bundle over to Paul. She watched him with a lump in her throat, aware of the symbolism in giving over the baby to him. *Please take care of him. He's yours now too.*

He was looking down at the fuzzy little head with tender fascination. 'It's really incredible, isn't it?' he said huskily, and her eyes grew misty at the love and wonder in his eyes. She loved the sight of the two of them—the big, gentle man and the small, helpless infant.

A few minutes later a nurse's aide came in to take the food tray away. She was round and cheerful with big brown eyes and a wide friendly mouth. 'My, my,' she said, smiling down at the baby in Paul's arms, 'don't he look the spittin' image of his daddy!'

Over the woman's curly head, Paul's eyes smiled at Kristin. She smiled back mistily. 'Just like I wanted,' she said.

An epic novel of exotic rituals
and the lure of the Upper Amazon

THE TAKERS RIVER OF GOLD

JERRY AND S.A. AHERN

THE TAKERS are the intrepid Josh Culhane and the seductive Mary Mulrooney. These two adventurers launch an incredible journey into the Brazilian rain forest. Far upriver, the jungle yields its deepest secret—the lost city of the Amazon warrior women!

THE TAKERS series is making publishing history. Awarded *The Romantic Times* first prize for High Adventure in 1984, the opening book in the series was hailed by *The Romantic Times* as "the next trend in romance writing and reading. Highly recommended!"

Jerry and S.A. Ahern have never been better!

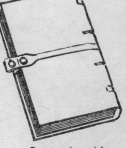